As
Told
By Monk

Joe Colicchio

DEDICATION

Well, four dedications:

Mom and Dad, Josie and Jack Colicchio, first.

All my friends from JC. When I was writing this book I thought of it as a love letter to a place and its people. I still do. It's a love letter to you.

And all my friends from my years in Massachusetts, the years during which I wrote *Monk*. I don't think I'd ever have written it without your support, love, and laughter. They were wonderful years.

The final dedication has to go to my boys Roy and Jack – I'm so proud of you and happy you get this glimpse into the old man – and to my wife Pat whose love and support, and whose encouragement of my writing efforts, has sustained me for many years now.

———————

The "original" *Monk* contained an epigram quoting Bruce Springsteen. Here's a more recent one: "The older you get, the more it means."

COLICCHIO

Punchball

We play ball mostly every day down at the courts. Stickball, basketball, boxball, and punchball. My favorite is punchball. You play it just like it sounds. You toss the ball in the air and you punch it. After you punch it you run the bases just like in baseball and hopefully you're safe.

I love standing on second with my hands on my knees, and I like rounding third on a single to the outfield. I like standing in the middle of center field watching and knowing what's going on.

Billy McCann, Boo, is probably the classic punchball player. Even though he's the smallest guy, only four foot eight, Boo's definitely the boss. You always have to call him when it's his turn to hit because he's never worried about it. He'll come up to home plate taking the wrapper off a piece of Bazooka or still talking to a girl sitting over on one of the cars. He looks the field over then goes into this trance. He closes his eyes and tightens his lips. He holds the ball in his left hand and punches it down to the ground, catches and punches, catches and punches, four, five, six times. Then he tosses the ball, takes two steps to catch up to it and Wham—going, going, it's outta here.

Then there's Mo Caruso. Mo's the best at all the things Boo doesn't do anymore, like stepping off people's shoes and climbing up the backboards. When you play punchball, you love Mo when he's on your team and hate him when he's not. Mo's style is that he's lefty and he's quick. He walks up to the plate with the ball in his right hand and his left hand behind his back, like a gentleman. He says things like Two on and two out and Mo Caruso at the plate. He squeezes the ball between his two middle fingers then pushes it out so when it hits the ground it bounces right back to him. He tries to lull the fielders into boredom or quick hit them before they're ready. He'll be just standing there with his head tipped towards the ground but his eyes straining up, inspecting the fielders' positions. Then all of a sudden he'll toss the ball just four or five inches into the air and try to cheap hit it to left field, chuckling all the way. Everybody says Mo plays like a Jap, but what Mo claims is that he's just smart and is using psychology.

And then there's Franny Gullace. Franny's my favorite. His father's dead. His mother cries a lot, he says. There are candles and rosaries and statues and things such like that all around the house. His house is a sad, sad place, and when Franny gets dark and his lips get red, he looks sad the same way. Every time Franny gets up to hit it's like the end of the world. Sometimes you think he's going to explode. He holds the ball cupped in his left hand and bangs and bangs it with his right. His knuckles turn white and the muscles in his neck bulge. When he makes good contact he hits it farther than anybody, Boo McCann included. But sometimes he doesn't get it right and hits the ball off his thumb or the bottom of his hand or off his wrist or sometimes misses it all together. When he does that he kicks the fire hydrant or smacks the telephone pole or does something else all red and furious, but one way or another, when he doesn't hit it the way he wants to he winds up hurting himself.

My name is Monk Fillipetti and I wear my red sweatshirt with a hood no matter how hot it is. My style is to hope and hustle. To play whenever I get choosed in and to watch when I don't. Today I played because it was Thursday. Thursdays the CYO takes trips to lakes and things so there are less kids around and I get to play.

We were tied in the bottom of the last, 14-14. Franny was on second cheating a lead and clapping his hands. It was my turn up, and Mo was in the on-deck circle talking to himself. Then the CYO bus pulled up across from Saint Paul's and who was the first one to come running off it waving his arms but the one and only Kenny Pepman. Like all hell busted loose two older guys on my team started yelling Monk's chucked, we chuck Monk, and shooing me away from home. But the other team grabbed me by both sleeves and dragged me back out and there was a big fight about whether or not I could be chucked. It was embarrassing. I didn't know what to do—if I should just stand there and watch them argue over me or if I should open my mouth.

SUMMER

Looking at Pictures

Our apartment above B&J Tavern is called railroad rooms. Harry and I have one bedroom. My mother and father have another. There's a living room in the front and a kitchen in the back. There are no doors between the rooms.

My mother was at Bingo last night, it was a Friday. My father was watching a Rawhide between falling asleep. Harry wasn't home yet. Him and his friends hang out on the church steps, then they go to Gregorio's for pizza before they get kicked out. Harry could take his time about it so long as he was home before my mother got back from Bingo.

It was lonesome in the house with my father half asleep and a bad Rawhide on TV. I missed my mother, the house felt empty without her. But I knew better than to tell anybody because then they'd say Monk's a baby.

I figured I'd do something. There was a box in the hall closet where we kept all our family pictures. It was a red box with white reindeers that my father got a sweater in two Christmases ago from my aunt on his side. I took the box down and went to my room. I sat at my desk and lit two candles and shut out the lamp. I put the box on my lap and started laying out the pictures on my desk. Some of the pictures were real old. Of my mother and father when they just got married and my mother was skinny and my father had longer hair. Some even of when they were kids. Some of dead people I never met. There were other pictures that weren't real old. Pictures of me and Harry and people who are also still alive.

I'd look at the pictures a minute and think, then lay them out in order on my desk. I don't remember what kind of order. But I'd look at them and say this one goes over there, that one there, this one between those two and so on and so forth. I'd move some straight and some not straight and some fast and some slow. Some I'd just rub round and round waiting for inspiration.

When Rawhide was over I heard my father get up and yell Monk, what are you doing in there. I said Nothing, Dad, just looking at pictures. He said Don't stay up too late in there now. I said No, Dad, okay. But I had all of these pictures set up in rows and was talking to them and holding conversations between them, laughing and crying for everybody.

The next thing I knew I heard Harry from his bed. He said Monk, are you going to stay up all damn night. I'm trying to fall asleep. I said Harry, it's you. I didn't even know you came in. He said I been laying here for almost an hour and said what were you doing when I came in. I said Oh, I'm sorry. I was listening to this music and didn't even hear you. He said Monk, you are once again confused. There isn't any music playing. I said to myself Monk, oh you stupid Monk. Maybe I was wrong, Harry said, I sneaked a couple of beers up at the park, don't tell. Maybe there was music before and you shut it off. I said, No, Harry, thanks. I remember now. It was me. It was me being stupid again. He said Don't worry. Just blow out the candles.

Religious Careers:
It Starts with Jeannie Simmons

Two months ago when the summer wasn't official even though the weather was hot and the clock turned ahead, I thought Jeannie Simmons was my girlfriend. It all happened on the bus ride back from Vocations Seminar Day at Seton Hall in Orange.

They take all the boys and girls from the fourth grade there to hear speeches by priests, nuns, and brothers of different orders, to sing and to collect pamphlets telling you where to write for information about the Calling. This year was our turn to go.

Jeannie and Mark DeFrio had been going out until that day. But when on the bus ride back Mark sat next to Peggy Enright and talked to no one but her, that was it. He hadn't spent much time with Jeannie even when he had a hundred chances to, walking around from booth to booth reading about the Bon Secours nuns and the Jesuits and Franciscans and Capricorns.

Jeannie was pretty sad when we got to the bus even before seeing Mark with Peggy. She seemed very tired and even more blue-veined than usual. She sat next to me because it was the only seat available at the front of the bus far away from Mark and the rest of that bunch. At first she didn't say anything to me, just Hi, Monk. I said Hi, also. I looked out the window thinking about her eyes and thinking that we probably weren't going to talk anymore.

Jeannie was the skinniest girl in the class. Fifty-six pounds in October on the school nurse's scale. She was very sick. So sick that no one made fun. She usually didn't get to school until at least ten minutes after the bell and her parents always drove her. She had the biggest green eyes I've ever seen. Sometimes they look the same color as shamrocks and sometimes they look pale. Ever since I met her in the second grade I wanted to tap her on the shoulder and say Jeannie, I think your eyes are great. But I was afraid it was all her pills and medicines and whatever they did to her in the hospital that made them colored the way they were. She coughed a lot and always had extra handkerchiefs to spit in. At school, at least once a week, she'd start gagging on her own phlegm and have to run out of class either red and laughing or crying.

Half way home on the bus coming back from Vocations Seminar Day she said Monk, what did you think of it? I said It was okay. Would you like a peanut butter cup? She said I'd love one. I took the Reese's out of the pouch in my sweatshirt and could tell right away it would stick to the paper, but it was too late. I handed it to her and I said I'm sorry, it's gooshy. I bought it at lunch and it's been in my pouch. She said It's okay. Are you sure you don't want any? And I said, No, thanks, I already had two.

Sister Ellen in the Convent

Not only didn't she hit kids, but Sister Ellen was the prettiest nun in the school. No question about it. So pretty in fact that the eighth grade boys said they got hard-ons when they thought about her.

I was sitting in the Courts yesterday, just a very regular Wednesday, watching a game when she called to me from Hancock Avenue. I ran down there to where she was giggling for no reason and leaning against the fence. She said There are a few things that have to be moved in the convent, Monk, do you think you could help me out for a little while. I said Sure, Sister. The church is right on Hancock Avenue, half a block from the Courts. The convent is on one side and the rectory on the other. Certain people, like Harry for instance, say the nuns and priests do it together, but I don't know about that.

Me and Sister Ellen went down to the basement of the convent which was very cool and two shades of green. One entire room was full of statues—Sacred Hearts, Saint Judes for Hopeless Causes, Ladies of Fatima. I couldn't help but thinking what a great stand this would have made at Palisades Park. I didn't have to move any statues, though. What I had to move was soup mostly, soup and some pork and beans. Shelves and shelves of Campbell's. It was a letdown.

Sister Ellen said they were getting a ping-pong table and a dart board and that this was going to be a Rec Room. She said she would consolidate the rows of statues and that I should put the soup where she made space. I carried six cans per trip, four on the last one, eleven trips in all. She said Monk, you're a fine worker. I said Thank you, Sister, I'll be glad to help any time, just don't be afraid to ask. She said Would you like some cookies. I said Sure, but it's alright. Never mind, she said, come up to the top floor balcony and I'll get you some.

The balcony overlooked the garden between the school and people's backyards. A fountain and three statues with little pools were in the garden. This was the first time I ever saw Sister Ellen's face in the sun. She tipped her head back and shut her eyes and took her glasses off. She said Monk, what's your real name. I said Daniel, but everybody calls me Monk. She hunched over and leaned in like a girl about to make a secret. She said I'll think of you as Daniel, Monk, if you think of me as Susan. I said You can think of me as Daniel but I don't think I can think of you as Susan. I could see her hair. It was the color of sand. It was peeking out of her habit, parted in the middle, exactly alike on either side. For a count of twelve, she didn't look at me, but kept her head tipped back with the sun pouring into it.

Then she looked down at the table, then at me, then at the garden. She said Aren't you hungry. I said Yes and ate some cookies. She said I wasn't always Sister Ellen. The sun lit up the sockets of her eyes and I could see the skinny blue veins in her bottom eyelids. She reached her hand back inside her collar and fluffed the black kerchief part of her habit like a princess fluffing her long hair. It hung a second in the breeze and separated into all its thin veils. The sun shone through them and made shadows you could barely make out waving across her cheek before they plopped back down around her head and shoulders as dark and solid as ever.

I ate the cookies and gulped down some of the milk. I said I wasn't always Monk, either. Into her hand she laughed, trying to make it seem like a cough. She said Monk, I think you're a real joy. And I said Sister, I think I'll go.

Mo the Magnificent

We sit on the Caruso's porch just about every night we don't stand around outside the Courts. Tonight we were all sitting there talking about Betty Keets. Mo was doing most of the talking and even though he's a good guy, once he gets going about Betty you can forget it for the rest of the night. One by one, everybody had just drifted off, so by ten o'clock it was just me and Mo sitting there.

Mo said Betty's tits are so big that some nights when she stands na-ka-ka-ked by the window you can see the n-n-n-nipples from his room. I started to ask a question but he answered it before I could get it out. Some nights they're bigger than others, he said. I said I don't think she's home, Mo. I've been looking in her window for most of an hour and I haven't seen a thing. He said that's because she's a whore. Do you know what a whore is, Monk. I said Sure, I know. She's no good. Mo said My father told me she's a baller from way back. That was a word I had never heard before but I more or less figured it out. She's got a daughter who's thirteen but doesn't live with her anymore and Mo said his father said She's a little baller already.

All of them clutching their pocketbooks, the ladies were waddling past on their way home from bingo. They were strung out down the block in gabby little groups of two and three. When they get out together like this on a Friday or Saturday night, they make the whole neighborhood stink of perfume. I appreciated that my mother knew enough to walk on the other side of the street and not embarrass me.

In a little bit I said I better get going. My mother wants me home by the time she gets there. I jumped off the porch and slammed the gate. Hey, Monk, said Mo, wait a second. I got a question for you. How come you never call me Mo the Magnificent. I said I don't know. How come you never call me Monk the Magnificent. How come you call me plain Mo, not the Magnificent like Slicer and Franny and Boo and everybody. I said I call you Motorman. I think it's a good nickname because you're so fast. He said Well, from now on I think you should call me Mo the Magnificent. I said Okay, fine. That's fine Mo the Magnificent.

So now I call him Mo the Magnificent whenever I get the chance. I figure if he likes it, I might as well. You know, the funny thing is that nobody ever calls Mo, Mo the Magnificent. Not ever. They call him plain Mo. That's all. He just thought the whole thing up himself.

From Asbury Park:
More with Jeannie Simmons

The last time I ever saw Jeannie was at the beach down Asbury Park while I was there on vacation with my parents and Jeannie was doing the same thing with hers. I saw her on the third day and was supposed to see her again on the fourth but the Simmonses didn't show up which bothered me then and still bothers me now and even more considering what happened a few days later.

We'd left Jersey City on Monday, the first day of my father's vacation and came home that Friday. So I can get it over with quick, my father said, and get at least a couple of days of peace before going back to that damned sweatshop. We stayed at the Flamingo Motel which is new and air-conditioned and pink and only two blocks from the beach and has its own postcards at the front desk like something you'd expect from Florida.

It rained on Monday afternoon when we got there and my father made me play rummy with him because my mother was watching the game shows and I was getting on their nerves—telling them what a good place the arcade would be to spend a rainy afternoon every two minutes which they claimed was every thirty seconds. It didn't take me long to get tired of playing rummy, but I pretended I wasn't so my father wouldn't just go out to a bar.

There's something sickening about playing rummy on the bed in a damp and dim and too air-conditioned room on a rainy day that's supposed to be the first day of your vacation at the shore. After I won fifty cents from him, my father decided to take a nap and made me write Flamingo Motel postcards which was even more sickening because we just got there and I had nothing to say. Who would?

The second day was real different. It was 85 by ten o'clock and hit 96 by 1:30. My parents were no more exciting than usual even though we were on vacation, but they were at least being agreeable with one another. Every half hour on the button, my mother would Phew and say I'm sweating bullets, Jack, and my father would say Yeah, it's a scorcher, what time is it. They'd say the same thing over and over and over but neither of them would say I'm bored. But by 1:30, I was ready to leave the beach and after nagging them for almost an hour we left around half past two.

By four o'clock we were back on the boardwalk mostly to get out of the room but also looking for food even though none of us were really hungry. It was still so scorching hot that I could feel the heat coming right up through my sneakers because I had no socks on. There were some families just going onto the beach and the water looked so blue and refreshing that I thought they must have been smarter families than we were and that it was my fault. I thought for sure that my mother and father were both blaming me for making them leave so early and that that was the only thing keeping them agreeable on such a hot day.

The third day was the way it was supposed to be. A good beach day, but not a burner. We were walking along the beach looking for a good spot when my mother stopped dead in her tracks and said Look, Monk, the Simmonses. My heart started thumping when I saw skinny Jeannie laying out there in her aqua bathing suit. I pretended it was no big deal. The mothers waved and the fathers walked towards one another with their heads down as though they would get to hand-shaking distance by radar and me and Jeannie fell into being the background. I realized it was a tricky situation but I did what I wanted to do and put my blanket down next to hers.

The first thing I wanted to ask her was how long she was going to be down for but I hesitated and she beat me to it. Until either Friday or Saturday I said nodding towards my father. She said she was going to be down until Sunday and that made me feel much better than if she was just down for the day because now I had more time to get her to like me.

After a little while of digging around in the sand with no particular purpose I asked her if she wanted to go in the water. She said Yeah, but I could see she wasn't too thrilled about it. When we got down there she stopped before she even got in up to her bathing suit. She put her hands on her hips like she was mad at herself and all determined but she couldn't stop from crying anyway. When she stopped enough that she could talk she explained to me about being sick. She named what it was she had and it was either a few big words or one extremely big word. While she did I was looking at her face which had two welts filled with reserve tears under her eyes and was still very nice looking, but I kept thinking of her chest which was caved in and her back which was hunched and which all together had a very squished in feeling. She said something about not being able to go any further into the water because if she swallowed more than a couple of mouthfuls it might drown her lungs, which as you might be able to tell I didn't really understand. But I nodded my head and asked her if she wanted to play catch instead. She said Yeah and ran back to the blanket as fast as she could to get the ball.

She wasn't a good thrower and only a little better at catching, but she was really trying and having a good time for a while, too. I kept getting closer and closer to her because I could see that the more we threw the more pale and tired she was getting. I started throwing underhand because each time she had to run after the ball she got hunched a little more.

One time when she was moving to catch a throw, she slipped and fell face-first into the sand. I got scared and ran over to her, but she was okay and we both laughed because of the sand she had stuck all over her. Her father must have heard us laughing and looked up. He let out this angry, angry yell. Jeannie, for God's sake, what in the hell are you trying to do. Get over to the blanket and lay down. I hung my head to avoid looking at my mother and father who I was sure would be siding with hers. I sat down next to Jeannie. She was so worn out and crying so hard that I thought for sure she was going to choke to death. I felt guilty that I was the one who made her run around and get tired like that, but I was mad at her father, too, because I didn't see any reason why he had to yell at her like he did. I know why he was upset, even shaking, but what good would yelling do.

When Jeannie got calmer she laid on her stomach with her arms at her sides. I looked at her fingers which were spread out, palms to the blanket. There were tiny centers on all her nails which must have been clear nail polish because it couldn't have been water but reminded me of tears. And then it blurted out and I yelled at her father. She was trying to play catch, that's all she was trying to do, I said and sat there looking for something to happen. But they didn't do anything except slump, looking at the sand between one another, having nothing to say. I got up and walked towards under the boardwalk because I couldn't take Jeannie's wheezing getting louder and louder and the five of us just sitting there like puppets with broken strings.

Watching Basketball One Week

The Summer Rec League started June 28th and continued until August 10th. The first game started each night at 5:30 and was for the Junior Division guys, 16-18 years old. I knew quite a few of them by name and some of them knew me. The big game each night was for men over 18. The Senior Division. Mostly these were guys who played basketball in college—Seton Hall, Jersey City State, Rutgers, St. Peter's College. There were other guys even older than them who some unfamiliar grown-up standing along the sidelines said played mostly in New York and that they were money players.

We'd make sure to get there by halftime of the first game. There weren't any seats around the court except for the folding beach ones that the Central Avenue Bernstengels, the Miragliottas, and the Red Kaufmans brought. If you were young and short, the only way you could get to see was to be right up on the sidelines. By getting there early you were sure to have a good spot. We'd sit at half-court on the Cambridge

Avenue side so we wouldn't have the setting sun to look into all two games.

It was a mystery why, but one night Boo McCann brought an orange with him. He said he had just finished supper that this was his dessert and that the fruit acid helped his indigestion. The next night Boo and Mo both brought fruit, Boo another orange and Mo a pear. By the third night, we all sat there watching the game and eating fruit and Boo brought cellophane. In addition to me and those two, the kids were Nehru and Draino and Slicer and Crabman. The fruits were oranges, pears, plums, grapes, cherries, and slices of watermelon and plain melon. It became a big thing, who would be the first to bring a new fruit. When Franny Gullace brought a plastic bowl filled with cherries, strawberries, and two kinds of grapes, even Boo was impressed. Personally, I had been nervous about bringing something different like that because usually I make out better if I just try to be not too noticeable.

I got my courage up, though, one night after confession and decided to try my luck. I didn't take anything from home, but coming to the Courts I stopped at the fruitman's. I realized that the one normal fruit that no one had brought was a banana, and, yes, it was a mistake.

I got there late because it had taken me so long to pick. I sat down with everybody and didn't say a word. Just matter of factly started peeling my banana. They looked at me and then looked at one another and started giggling like a bunch of second grade girls. Obviously it was very funny to be eating a banana in public but I didn't get it. Boo said How's the banana, Monk. I said It's good, I bought it, and they laughed some more. A couple of minutes later when I pulled another one out from my waist, Boo asked again and they laughed again. I felt stupid without knowing why (which wasn't unusual) and thought for sure that all hundred people there were looking at the boy eating a banana at a basketball game. But still I started a third one. Boo said Boy, you must really love bananas, Monk. I said, I do. I just thought it was something different and a perfectly good fruit.

Just then, Fred Cucci showed up and saved me from this mess. He sat down and when everybody saw what he was eating started laughing so hard that I had to start laughing, too, even though I still couldn't figure out what was so funny. They were all laying on their backs, screaming and yelping, pulling their hair, smacking the sides of their heads, and making such a scene that three of the players looked over to see what the ruckus was. Boo said Fred how's the pickle. Freddy said Good, it's dill. And when he heard the word Dill tears started pouring out the eyes of Franny Gullace. Boo said Fred I hate to say this, but you're dumber than Monk. A pickle isn't even a fruit.

I thought this was great because it took me off the hook and because they said someone was dumber than me, so I said Dill and laughed.

As it turned out like everything else it wasn't a hundred percent good because Fred who is a good kid and just got left back couldn't take the idea of being dumber than me. Real quiet, he just laid his pickle right on the ground, got up and started walking away. After a few steps we could see his back humping and we knew he was crying. Jesus H. Christ, I thought. He started running and ran straight across the court and out the gate, his back humping all the way.

Wake Parish

One day, all of a sudden, after it had been beautiful out the whole morning, it started pouring. Everybody raced from the courts shrieking like it was the end of the world. The rain was splashing so hard you could see it pop back up after it hit the street. The water slid in sheets and tiny waves and over-ran the sewers. All the cars had their headlight on and moved like zombies.

Because I lived upstairs and my father was his friend, Joe McGill let me stay down in B&J's even though kids weren't usually allowed. Joe listened to WVNJ every afternoon and it must have been the most boring station in the world. He pulled a stool over to the corner of the bar and gave me a soda and some pretzels for nothing and some napkins to dry my face.

The bar got crowded quick with all these wet men running in and after ten minutes the place was so foggy that Joe had to open the door. It was really something to look outside where now the sun was shining even though the rain was still smashing down, like you were in a fish bowl only opposite. The rain was pep-pep-pepping off the awnings and the entire Zawodowicz family was yelling for Blood, their dog.

Wake Parish, who was sitting two or three seats down from me, winked and said How's the folks, Monk. I said Good, Wake, how are you. He said Fine, tell them I was asking for them. I said Sure and tell Cotton I was asking for him, too. Wake wore a lot of greens and browns, and he had very neat brown hair even though it was a little longer on his neck than most guys. He'd become real friendly with Mr. Simmons lately and had started asking me about Jeannie in a way that always made me feel like I wasn't telling him enough. I remember my father talking to a bunch of guys not too long ago and he said Wake's really a gentle one, very gentle. Now Monk I don't mean anything by that. Joe McGill said There's something about him, I can't put my finger on it, not necessarily bad but I don't know. And my father said Maybe he's a little confused, you know, pent up, here, but he's gentle, even sad or something here.

Wake turned to me again and said I gotta go up to Pershing Field, Monk, feel like taking a walk. It was a bright, beautiful day, steam coming off the black. I said Sure, Wake, I'm done with my soda. He said Good, why don't you go up and put on a dry sweatshirt and make sure with your mother it's okay.

We walked along Cambridge which is the way those guys always walked because they said it was shorter even though that made no sense to me. We didn't talk much. Not about anything. That was fine with me and seemed fine with Wake, too.

At the corner of Cambridge and Bowers, we met this dog, a skinny black and white mutt, that I made the mistake of bending over to pet and giving some crumbs from my pouch to. When we got to Hutton Street, the dog was still following us and that was a problem because Hutton Street is a big two-way street and from the looks of him that dog could have never made it across without getting hit. Me and Wake looked at one another. Wake surprised me when he said Well, we'll just have to wait him out. He sat down and I did, too. The dripping-wet dog looked like he had nowhere to go. He just laid right out with us. Whenever we stood up to try to get away, he stood up also. We had no escape.

After fifteen minutes of looking back and forth at the mutt, I got the feeling that Wake would sit there all day and never mind about getting to Pershing Field. Well, finally, I got up and I stomped my foot three times at the dog, each time a little bit closer, and yelled yah-yah-yump, get outta here. The dog got up and started trotting down the block as best he could, every once in a while looking back at us over his shoulder. I looked at Wake and was he ever steaming. That was wrong, Monk, that was a wrong thing to do what you did, he said. I expected better, I did, he said. He got up and started chasing after the dog, whistling, skipping between the steps he walked and the ones he ran.

I felt miserable, like the worst rat in the world. I looked down at the wet spot on the ground where the dog had been laying and wished it would hurry up and dry so I could get going back to the Courts.

Three Stories from the Same Day: Jeannie Simmons

1)

When I left the house this morning, it seemed a lot earlier than it really was, 9:30. Things usually start getting pretty hot and white around here by then, but this morning had the kind of coolness to it that's usually gone by eight. Mrs. Draimis was just hanging out her clothes. The pulley was squeaking so you could hear it from a block away sounding like a dying bird and the clothes were rocking back and forth over her hedges. Things were very slow. There was a breeze rustling the trees and it seems like there was lots of shade. It would have been a perfect morning for sitting with Franny and Freddy and Mo, reading the sports, talking and waiting and wrestling. As I walked towards the church it seemed more like spring than summer and reminded me of Easter more than anything else.

2)

After the funeral, I took the incense and the silver incense burner out to the yard behind the rectory, something the altar boy always does, and I was kneeling down, burying the incense in the dirt and looking out through the alleyway between the rectory and the church at all the people milling around out front. I was thinking sad and awful thoughts about

26

Jeannie. I was picturing what she looked like not so long ago when she was alive and picturing what she must have looked like inside the shiny casket—but that was too much and I had to shut off that picture quick. I was thinking I was lucky to be here in the back where I could think for myself instead of being out there milling with all those people when I felt someone tap me on the shoulder. I looked up and there standing over me was Mr. Simmons, all red around the nose and eyes, his eyeballs a kind of sticky wet. He reached out with a five dollar bill because that's something they always do after you serve a funeral.

He said I should take it and split it with Bob, Jeannie's cousin from Fairview who'd come all the way in to serve the mass. I told Mr. Simmons No. He crumbled the bill and stuffed it back into his pocket without arguing. Then he knelt right down next to me even though he was in a black suit. I could hear him sobbing and see the little trembly motion of his back, but I couldn't see his face because of the way his chin was tucked in against his chest. He put his hand into the hole I'd been digging and he started digging himself. He put his hand into the burner and pulled some incense out and started burying that in the hole, hiding his face all the time.

There was something about it that kept me from feeling anything. You'd think that I would have felt something—sad for Jeannie or Mr. Simmons, or at least felt scared or upset or at least something. But all I could do was lean away and watch stiff and clenched and without a thought in my head. I looked up and through the alleyway at all the dressed up people, all of them in little groups or walking around in circles looking for someone, and they all looked like they were made of thin air and I got dizzy.

Father Ward called me from the sacristy and I jumped up. I stood to go over there but didn't know what to do about Mr. Simmons and the burner. I tapped him on the shoulder and said Mr. Simmons, Father Ward's calling me, can I have the incense thing. Yeah, he said, yeah, oh yeah sure, Monk. He placed the cap on the burner and handed it to me. I guess I should be out front, he said. I guess that's where I should be. I guess what I'm supposed to say is how sad I am but I'm relieved in a way. I said I wouldn't know. He said I'm not relieved. I'm not relieved at all. I'm sick with what's like a poison all through me, Monk.

Father Ward called again and Mr. Simmons said You better get going before you get thrown off the force. He said he was going out front because him more than anyone was supposed be there receiving their prayers and their She's in heaven with God nows.

As I was running up the steps to the sacristy, very careful to hold onto the burner with both hands, Mr. Simmons yelled to me. Hey, Monk, if you or Father notice any more mistakes the Good Lord's made, just let me know. You just let me know and I'll see what I can do about fixing them.

3)

There were only four cars in the procession from Saint Paul's to Holy Name Cemetery. In the first car were Jeannie and four men in black uniforms who carried the casket. In the second car, a long grey Chevrolet, the only car that wasn't black, was Mr. and Mrs. Simmons. In the third car was Father Ward and Bob and me. In the fourth car, a station wagon, were seven nuns, including Sister Ellen.

As we pulled up to the gates of the cemetery, the

first car stopped and the driver spoke to a man in a blue uniform inside a booth who gave him directions. The driver made a left on a road called Saint Jude Lane. (Personally, I thought it was odd that they'd put addresses on gravestones.) We drove off the road and onto a field which was a lot less crowded than the other areas since it hadn't been lined with rows and rows of gravestones yet. There were two men in tan work clothes with shovels waiting for us there.

The four men got out of Jeannie's car and moved around to the back without saying a word. They opened the back door of the hearse and grabbed onto the handles of the short casket and pulled Jeannie out leaving me wondering which end was her feet and which her head. They carried her over near the two men with the shovels and placed her down next to the hole there. Everybody gathered around and folded their hands on their bellies, except for two of the nuns who folded their hands right up under their chins. Father Ward told Bob to grab the gold bucket with the holy water and he cupped the back of our heads in his hands and led us over to where we should be, right behind the casket.

The seven nuns stood across the ditch from us. Up at the head of the ditch were Mr. and Mrs. Simmons with their bodies pushed against one another's. They'd look up at the sky and huff, then straight ahead and cry, then down to the ground and whisper or pray. But they never looked at the same place at the same time. It was as though their heads were on a sort of hinge that made one move up as the other moved down.

Just as Father Ward was about to start, another car pulled up, a beat up green Dodge and out came Wake Parish. He had his hands in his pockets and the collar of his shirt turned up like he was chilly, but even though it was mostly overcast it still must have been seventy-five degrees out. He was wearing a red arm band. I really don't know why he came, but as far as I know there aren't laws about who can and can't be at a burial so whatever Wake's reasons were they were his business and nobody had the right to say otherwise. He didn't look at anyone when he came over but just stood a little off to the side, between where we were and the ducks waddling around by the pond. He hung his head so Father would continue.

Father Ward opened his prayerbook and nodded at the four men from Jeannie's car who picked her up and lowered her into the hole. Father Ward started. Sometimes he'd look in his book and read Latin and bless himself in that way where you keep your hand stiff and move it up then down then left then right without touching yourself. Other times he'd look up and around and talk English. He nudged Bob to hand him the holy water sprinkler, but Bob didn't budge. His face and neck were splotchy red from nerves. His sideburns were wet and came to a point. Father Ward had to reach over and take the bucket from Bob's hand and give it to me. He held the sprinkler up in his right hand and was about to spritz the casket when he caught himself and made me and Bob switch sides because there's something about which side you take the holy water from and I guess he didn't want to take any chances.

Everybody stood there watching and listening and Father talked and sprinkled. After a few minutes Wake moved around from one side of the hole to the other where he was mostly behind the nuns and the Simmonses wouldn't be able to see him. He was rocking back and forth, head tipped, hands folded on his belt buckle.

Father ended the service with a moment of silence—which the ducks messed up bad—and then a regular sign of the cross. As soon as it was over, the four men in black uniforms hustled over to their car like there was some place they had to get to in a hurry. The seven nuns moved right up to the edge of the hole and knelt down and peered in. They pulled out their rosary beads and went at it like a bunch of starving orphans. Wake threw his red armband in the grave then left without so much as a genuflect. Mr. and Mrs. Simmons came over to Father Ward and they stood talking, both of Father's hands on each of theirs together in a single grip.

Meanwhile, me and Bob wandered around reading the gravestones. Bob was handling things a little better than before but still he'd get these terrible shivers all up and down his body. The first time he shivered I did it too, I think because I was embarrassed for him but it must have been contagious because after a couple I wound up shivering whenever he did without even trying to.

When we came back to Jeannie's final resting place, they'd all left—the nuns and Mr. and Mrs. Simmons. All who were left around the hole that was going to be 12 Saint Jude Lane were me and Bob and Father Ward (and Jeannie, if you count her) and the two men in tan uniforms leaning on their shovels.

On the Roof During a Heatwave

There are some nights when my father lets Harry and me sleep out on the roof. My mother has the ropes on most things that we can and can't do, but I guess because sleeping on the roof is an outside thing, and she only seems to have control of things inside the house, dad gets to say when we can and when we can't.

We were in the middle of the summer's worst heatwave, Tuesday hit 103, and the rest of the days were close to it. My mother spent the whole day sitting in the shade under the Pavone's tree with Annie and some other ladies all sitting or standing there rocking their strollers, my mother just fanning herself and complaining about how sticky the nights were. When my father got home at around 5:30, he parked the car then walked over to where they were all gabbing there. He kidded my mother about having some racket while he was out working all day. He worked in an industrial laundry which was a lot more like a factory than a laundromat and was the hottest place I've ever been. His sleeves were rolled up and his arms were sweaty and greasy. He stood over my mother. Don't touch me, Jack. Don't you dare touch me. And my father said Well, Tootsie, how about getting that rear end of yours upstairs and making some supper. Mrs. Pavone said Leave her alone, Jack, she just came down. Better days are coming, my father said. Don't worry, Annie, better days are coming.

After supper, Harry went over to the Miragliotta's to smoke on their garage roof, but I just sat on the porch playing Seven Pack Solitaire. My mother and father came back down under the Pavone's tree. My mother wound up sitting there all night like she did just about every night, drinking Tab or beer and gabbing, naturally. My father never really got interested in all the ladies' talk. He'd wind up having to ask What, what was that you were saying when someone asked him a question. Sometimes they'd deliver the punch line to a joke and he'd laugh like he knew what they were talking about.

He stood and said I'm going up, gals, and winked at my mother like it was fine for her to stay down for as long as she wanted. When he went upstairs, I did too and we sat in front of the TV, me on the floor, him in his chair drinking Tom Collinses that I mixed.

When my father finally decided to go to sleep Harry and me were both already in bed. He came walking by the door and heard me tossing and turning because of the heat. Our room was the hottest in the house because the fan was broke and because being in the middle of the house, it didn't get the breeze that my parents' did in the back. My father didn't even have to ask. All he had to say was If I was a young guy I sure wouldn't be sleeping in such a hot stuffy room. Then all I had to do was wake Harry and nod my head for him to get it, too.

The roof that we slept on was the garage roof. It was attached to our house and was only a couple of feet down from the window. When we slept outside, me and Harry kept our regular summer pj bottoms on. For tops, me and Harry each brought two T-shirts out, one of them a long-sleever just in case. We jumped out the kitchen window and laid our blankets and pillows down.

You could crawl to the edge of the garage roof

and look down onto the street without anyone being able to see you. Harry wasn't too interested in it but I was. Harry laid there with his arms folded across his eyes. His knees were bent and crossed as if he was sitting up. He always snored when we slept outside which I thought was very grown up for a thirteen year old but also weird. But me, I could just lay there all night and look at the cars passing and at the teenagers and the drunks and guys holding beer cans and making a racket outside B&J's, acting like a bunch of kids themselves.

By one o'clock the streets were empty but I still laid there looking. One by one the lights in all the houses blinked out. The streetlights threw shadows through the trees. Nothing moved except maybe the trees a little bit. The sounds were only once-in-awhile and far away—sirens, trains, a honking horn, a guy and girl fighting.

I started doing something pretty weird and got caught by Harry. I popped up and started pacing back and forth with my hands clasped behind my back as though I was fifty years old. I started motioning and nodding my head and taking long, slow strides and talking to myself even though there weren't any real words I could think of. Pretending I was saying very serious things but just Blahblah-blahblahblahing.

Once when I walked to the back edge of the roof over where B&J's kept their garbage I looked down and saw these two shining brown eyes looking back at me. We stood there looking at one another for a long time without moving until finally the brown eyes started barking up a storm. Harry sat up and said What the hell. You know, it's late, Monk. I said, Geez, that Lobue's dog is a loud one. Did you hear him? Get to sleep, Monk, for crying out loud, he said. Yeah, I said.

Before I did, though, I went to the front of the roof and looked around the corner and into my parents' room to see if the barking woke them. They were dead asleep—my mother laying on her stomach with a pillow over her head and my father stiff on his back with his mouth hanging open.

I came back and laid down but I still wasn't ready for sleep. I crawled to the edge of the roof and looked out over the street some more just imagining. A leaf fell from the Pavone's tree and dipsy-doodled past the streetlight. I felt a nice little breeze and knew that we were done with the heatwave.

Summer was almost over, a short ten days until Labor Day and school. But that was still okay. Because I knew I had next summer and the next one and the next one after that to look forward to. I folded my hands on my belly and looked up at the moon and stars, still pretending to be having serious thoughts.

EARLY FALL

Harry Rigamarolling Me

The only thing Harry kept saying the whole night and all morning before school, and all afternoon which started early because we only had half a day, was that it was no big deal. That the first day of school was no big deal and that I was being very immature for making such a big rigamarole about it. (One thing about guys going into the eighth grade is that they mature overnight.)

Well, this morning was the first day of school and without a doubt it was five degrees cooler than any morning of the whole summer. The house smelled of my new red sweatshirt still in its plastic and like mothballs and new shoes and pencils and bookbags which is certainly different from the way it usually smells in the mornings in the summer.

Finally Harry came out of the bathroom and sat at the table with me, pretending like he didn't have a care in the world. I said It feels pretty chilly this morning, doesn't it, Harry. About the same, in fact I'm kinda warm, he said and took off his t-shirt which my mother made him put right back on.

I said Who do you think you'll get?

Probably either Sister John or Miss Greco, he said and went right back to his eggs. Gimme the salt.

Well, who do you hope you'll get, I asked, still doing my best to be nice about it. He didn't answer, just kept chewing on his eggs like they were a steak.

Finally, he said How should I know. It doesn't matter anyway.

That's when we got into the fight.

My mother came in and told me to zip it and chased Harry from the table. He was dragging himself out like he had a lead ball chained to his leg but had to stop right over me to get two more Rigamarole-rigamaroles in, and I threatened him with my fork and my mother folded her arms and said Oh, I can see I'm going to have a ball with you two this year and Harry said He asks stupid questions. How am I supposed to know who I'm gonna get and slammed the bathroom door to spite me.

On the first day of school you always go to the last year's classroom and they tell you where to go from there. It's fun being in school after not being there for the whole summer. Everything seems littler. The bathroom smells sparkling clean. And the clothing room and the chalk and the erasers and the blackboard, and the statues and flags and Sisters smell so strong they almost choke you. And Walt Hanker smells the same every year and you can take my word for it everyone in class went up to him to get a whiff just to be sure. The teacher is always real friendly out of relief because she knows this is the last time she's ever gonna have to see all of you together, and you see all your buddies who you haven't seen all summer and stand off in some corner talking about everybody else and think they're all wondering what you're saying.

But you're kind of nervous, too, because this is the day that is going to decide who's in your class for the whole year. If the teacher reads off your name, you're in one class and stand against the wall. If she doesn't you're in the other. The only one of my good summer friends who was in my class last year was Franny Gullace who got left back in the third when his father died.

I was the first kid to be called for Sister Ellen's class even though I wasn't the first one alphabetically, and stood against the wall while Smack Sister Rita (otherwise known as Little Doom) read off the rest of the names. I think everybody was waiting to see if Little Doom would make a mistake so they could be the first to yell out that Jeannie was dead. But old Sister Rita just kept scratching and working down the page and never gave us a good excuse to laugh at her.

She called Franny's name and we smiled and nodded at one another when he joined me up there. Next she called Maria DiDinardo and when Franny heard her name he looked at me and put his hand over his heart like he was about to die and collapsed onto the floor where he squirmed around until Sister Rita stabbed him in the butt with her cane. All morning long, whenever he got the chance, and then all afternoon when we met at the courts, Franny complained about having to sit next to Bellina Facci because, he said, she was so ugly, which everybody said but wasn't true, and because she didn't let you cheat off her, which was.

As we were filing out, Sister Rita said to me You were supposed to be in the B reading group, but that decision, Mr. Monk, was changed. Not by me, rest assured. I hope you make the best of this turn of events. Which meant that for the first time in all my five years of school I was going to be in the fast reading group and that if I didn't do good I would probably never again get a chance. I said Thank you very much, sister. But Sister Rita who is an old and extremely itchy nun, never did like me and couldn't even bring herself to give me a You're welcome.

We went through the first day and Sister Ellen didn't say anything special to me or act like she had anything to do with me being in her class. She put me where I belonged alphabetically and ignored me as she went through the regular first day stuff.

The most unusual thing for me was Jeannie missing. For a few minutes all I'd be able to think about was her not being around. That wasn't the weird thing. But then a whole half hour would pass and I'd just get involved in talking or listening or staring up at the clock, and I'd forget she ever existed. That's an awful thing.

Then the bell rang. Day one was over.

When I saw Harry on the way home I was busy trying to get all the different smells from the morning straight in my head. I know it was a mistake to, but I said so to Harry. God, it smells the same every year, he said. You'll be used to it by the end of the week, just wait. I just snickered and brushed it off. Who'd you get, I asked. Miss Farrell, of course, he said. I knew I'd get stuck with her. I said I asked you this morning and you said how were you supposed to know. He said he had too known and stuck his underarm in my face and we got into another fight, me with my hood up and my hands over my ears and Harry rigamarole-rigamarolling me all the way home.

Mr. Caruso the Magnificent

Late this afternoon, Saturday, not being in a very good mood after not getting to play because a lot of older kids had taken over the courts for a football game you didn't want to get in the way of, I ran into Mr. Sam Caruso on my way home at a quarter to five.

Mr. Caruso smokes cigars, has a beer belly, a bald head, and a shiny face. He was sitting right in the middle of the sidewalk rubbing lotion onto himself, stretched out in a big lounge chair so that you practically had to go into the gutter to get around him. I said Hello and kept walking like I had somewhere to get to, but Mr. Caruso said Monk, come over here. There's something I want to talk to you about. Uh-oh, I thought, because for a man Mr. Caruso is the biggest yakker I've ever met.

Let me tell you something about yourself, he said. You're a very interesting and intelligent young man though not many think so. He put one handkerchief in one pants pocket and took a different one out from the other. He had some sort of oily lotion on his legs and he polished his knees then relit his cigar staring at the lit tip like it was rocket science. Well, I knew he intended to be talking for a while. He squished over so I could fit on the lounger. He grabbed onto one of my arms so he could squeeze whenever he wanted me to smile or nod or look at him. I bought this house in nineteen-hundred and forty-seven, five months after I got married. Right away I knew this was the end of me hearing anything about me being interesting and intelligent. I bought it for eight thousand. Today it would cost twenty (squeeze). I could have bought those other two right across the street, the Manente's and the Hookings' for another twelve grand and they would have thrown in garages on the corner for another three. But I didn't have the money (squeeze). That's all there is to it, Monk. I just didn't have the money, he said and leaned back for the first time. So I try to explain to Mrs. Caruso how that makes me the way I am today, but God forbid she should give any thought to what I have to say. See, that's human nature, he said (squeeze). Well, in April of the next year, a year to the month after we moved in, Mo's big sister Ninette was born, 8 pounds 8, a beautiful baby. That's what I keep telling Mrs. Caruso. (I might have been the one and only Miss Anthony Cleopatra for all he knew of who he was talking to.)

The rest of what he said went on pretty much the same way, only as interesting to you as you were in Mr. Caruso, meaning that mostly it was very and only interesting to him. But he told me the whole history, everything from breaking his ankle when he fell through the roof in 1952 to Mo getting caught in a sewer in 1956 when he was trying to get a ball out to the time he saved a dog from a raging house fire in 1959.

I was trapped with no way to get out until Harry came down at 5:30 to get me for supper. I got up to leave and Mr. Caruso put his cigar out on the sidewalk. Come talk to me any time you want, Monk. Like I said you're an interesting and intelligent fellow. Yeah, thanks, I said.

Off I went with Harry. I flicked him in the ear and warned him that there was a limit to my patience and that he better not tell any more adults that I wrote stories, sometimes about people in the neighborhood.

Breakfast in Donutland

Every Tuesday morning, instead of my mother making it herself, she lets me go down to Donutland for breakfast. It works out good for both of us because it's a change for me, coming in the middle of the week like that, and it's a change for her, too, and keeps me from getting on her nerves day after day. The only rules were No Coffee, No Coke, and if I was late for school even once the whole thing was off.

Yesterday morning, which was Tuesday morning, I had to bring down the milk bottles so went the back way and was cutting through B&J's when I bumped into Cotton Parish, Wake's brother. Even though him and Wake are brothers, they look and act as unlike one another as possible. Cotton's real name is Don. He got his name because his hair's like cotton candy, only not so pink. He seemed glad to see me and said Where are you going Monk. I said To Donutland for breakfast. He said You mind if I come. I said No, I'll enjoy the company. He said Let's run. That's another thing about Cotton. He always runs. Not because he's in a hurry, but just because he likes to. You know he's not in a hurry because if he sees you on the avenue or something he'll always stop to talk. And once he gets your ear like that, you might just as well sign away the next twenty minutes. When he leaves he says So long, and gives you his famous two-fingered salute. Within five steps he's off running like my father says he's run since he was a kid back in the days when the courts were just a vacant lot, his hands bouncing up and down in front of him and his head bobbing like the fake poodle in the back of the Lobue's car.

We didn't say a word to one another all along our run to Donutland, not until we sat down and each ordered our muffins. Mrs. Gullace, Franny's mother, was working behind the counter.

Dave who is the owner of Dolph's came bustling through the door like a cold white wind, his coat half still on him and half already hung up, and him huffing and puffing and coughing, bent over trying to rub the stain out of his gray pants. Hey, how are you today, Dave, asked Mrs. Gullace. Coffee, said Dave. Skim no sugar and a jelly donut and some extra napkins please he said in a single rush.

I tapped Cotton on the shoulder and shook my head and nodded it towards Dave so he knew what I thought was so funny and we both grinned. So anyway, he said, how's Wake been, Monk. I said I don't know, Cotton, he hasn't been around much lately—you're his brother. Cotton laughed and raised his eyebrows at that, and the hairs on his head seemed to stretch out a little bit as though they were laughing, too. He said Well, how was he the last time you saw him. I said The last time I saw him was before school started and he got real mad at me just for scatting a dog. Yeah, I know, said Cotton, your dad told me. He did, I said. Yeah, yeah. How did it make you feel. Well, I could tell you the truth, I said, if you won't mind it. I won't mind it, I'm interested, he said. Well, firstly, when he got so mad I was afraid he might hit me, then when he ran after the dog all upset I started thinking that maybe I really did do something awfully bad, but now when I think about it mostly I just worry about poor Wake.

Mr. Knopf hasn't been in yet, has he, Rose, asked Dave, patting the jelly off his mouth with real precision as though he knew exactly where the spots were. No, Dave, no, relax. Have some decaf, she said. Here, slow down. Thank you. And give me some more napkins, too, please, thank you. Mrs. Gullace did that and she leaned over to Dave with a wet cloth and dabbed jelly off his collar while Dave sat there as though nothing was going on, trying to drink his coffee on the other side of her two arms.

Why, what do you think about Wake, I asked Cotton. Yeah, I worry about him sometimes, he said and started bobbing his head just like when he ran. Has he yelled at you, too, I asked. Yeah, he has, he said and looked out the window. We yell at one another. And so what do you think about it. Finish your milk, he said and this surprised me because I thought the whole reason for him coming with me here was to talk about Wake, and we had started to, and pretty well, I thought, and now all of a sudden he didn't want to anymore. He raised his eyebrows and said It's not your worry, Monk.

So how goes it, Dave, asked Mrs. Gullace. I haven't seen you for a while. Oh, he said, very bad, we should be doing much better this time of year with school just back. We got a new style of Farah slacks that I'm selling for two dollars less than anyone in the city. All sizes, men and boys. He looked at me and Cotton and said Ten ninety-five and looked back at Mrs. Gullace. And what's wrong with the BVD brand. Nobody buys BVD anymore. What's the matter, BVD gives you plague all of a sudden. I wear BVD personally, they're a fine undergarment. Then Mrs. Gullace said Not the business, Dave. Not the business, how are you. Your heart. The doctor said I may need another operation. But he's very young, the doctor. I know we used to do much better up this avenue. It used to be a goldmine. Then he said it again, intended for us. We used to do much better up this avenue.

I looked at the clock and saw that it was almost 8:30. I said I gotta get going, Cotton. Fine, he said, let's blow. Cotton paid for mine. I thanked him and said good-bye to Mrs. Gullace and looked at and nodded at Dave who looked down at my pants and shook his head. When me and Cotton got to the sidewalk, I'm going this way, he said, going to the A&P. Look, don't worry about Wake. No, I know, I said. Just keep an eye on him, Cotton said, and let me know. If it wasn't so late I would have asked him what he meant because I thought he thought I understood something that I didn't. I said Sure, Cotton, see you, and we turned in opposite directions running to our destinations.

I tried running like Cotton with my hands bouncing in front of my chest and my head bobbing, so I turned around after a little bit to get another look. When I did, Cotton wasn't running towards the A&P, but was coming back, his head going back and forth instead of up and down. I was going to wave but didn't. I turned around and kept running to school.

On My Parents' Bed

Last Friday night, while my mother was at Bingo, my father and me laid on his and my mother's bed talking mostly about World War II which he was in. We were laying there since around 8:30, just after Rawhide ended. Like most things, it happened by accident because my father had been laying there in bed with the dim lamp light on trying to read the Daily News and I passed by in my pajamas because I was taking the long way to the bathroom not because we had planned to lay in bed and talk about things. In fact, the first thing my father said to me was They must be ready to start the full card, huh, Monk, meaning that they were about to start the Jackpot game and that my mother would be home in a little over half an hour. Yeah, I said, then they just have the T game.

We went from talking about Bingo to talking about the old days when the Giants and Dodgers were still in town to talking about World War II which is where my father wanted to get to all along. I sat on the edge of the bed with my bottom lip turned out just like my father and my chin resting on my shoulder so I could see him without killing my neck.

The rug ended where the bed began and I swung my feet back and forth, first brushing them along the rug then tapping them on the slightly sticky linoleum under the bed where I pretended serpents lurked. Hey, should I tell you more stories about me in World War II like we did that other time, my father asked. I said, Yeah, sure, do you want me to get you a ball and a beer. Yeah, good idea, he said, and don't forget to wash the glass.

I came back with a good head on the beer and the whiskey bottle and shot glass in my other hand. I put it all down then sat next to him at the top of the bed. He was in the Navy in this telling instead of the Air Force because, he said, the Navy needed a few good men with his background to help the Limeys against the Nazi U-boats in the North Atlantic. I would have preferred the South Pacific, I said, just for the water temperature. There's no preferring in the military, not in wartime. In one mission, he said, when they were chasing half a dozen of these U-boats through the English Channel, they came head to head with the mighty Bismarck, a battleship so fearsome a movie came out about it. He put his hands up like binoculars around his eyes, and made like he spotted the Bismarck through the window. He took a shot (a shot of whiskey) then turned out the lamp so we wouldn't give our position away. He grabbed me by the arms and made like they were the handles on one of the big revolving guns on the ship's deck and rat-tat-tatted me around the room. In addition to doing the rat-tat-tatting, he also did the fusss-sussssssing of the torpedoes whizzing past, the burrrrooo-burrrrooooming of the bombs falling and the grgrgrgrgrgring of all the German fighter jets which suddenly appeared overhead and which he was shooting me at. Then he let go of me with one hand. He took another shot then started turning the lamp light on and off real fast, spinning me back and forth til I was lopsided and doing some rat-tat-tatting myself. It was quite a thing.

We both looked up at the same time and saw my mother standing in the doorway. She had a twinkle or something in her eye that I don't remember noticing before and I thought she might have won the jackpot.

No, I didn't win any jackpot, she said, I lost again. She made a fake sad face at my father who made a fake sad face back and said Poor mommy. He said Why don't you join your two men on the bed and listen to my daring exploits of 1943. She said Pffft and waved her hand and started walking out the door and that said it all. My father said Where you going, tootsie. And she said I'm all sweaty. They had a problem with the heat. I was stuck in a corner where heat was coming up. I've got to take this girdle off and put on some powder and get into something comfortable and then she waved her hand again at something my father did behind my back.

I started feeling creepy so asked my father if he wanted another beer and after he said Yes I got it and stood in front of the refrigerator for a couple of seconds. I came back and poured and sat at the bottom of the bed. I decided to just sit there until my mother came out of the bathroom and then I could go in and just leave those two alone.

She came over to the bed and tried to lift me, thinking she'd carry me to my bedroom, but now that I'm almost 70 she had a lot of trouble with the lifting and just plopped me back onto the mattress. Then, like a picture, we stayed like that—my father sitting up with his legs stretched out and his big toenail cutting through his white sock, me in a heap in my one corner, my mother standing there looking, proud and all.

My father stretched his arm out for my mother. Come here, mom, he said. She leaned down and kissed the old man on the lips and pushed herself away. She sat on the bed next to me. She fell onto her back when she tried leaning over to touch me and wound up kissing the spot on my arm where my dad had been rat-tat-tatting me. Then my father ran his hand through my hair as gently as my mom usually does and squeezed my neck. Alright, already.

I pulled my feet up on to the bed waiting for a good time to leave, and happier than I'd like to explain that it was a chilly night and I had underwear on beneath my pajamas.

The Safest Way

If you stretch your right arm out straight above your head and stretch your left arm out, too, and bend it at the elbow so the back of your hand slides under your head in the cradle they make, you can sleep on your stomach without suffocating and that way avoid dying in the middle of the night like many people have before you.

Blessed in Latin

If you think it's dark and hard getting up for school, you should try getting up for 6:30 mass. It was the first week of October. That with the clocks still on their summer schedules, even though it gets dark later at night, it stays dark later in the morning, too, is something I think few people, including farmers and altar boys, really understand.

To make it on time to serve the 6:30, you have to get out of bed at 5:30 when the world is still in utter darkness. My mother came in to get me up. I could hear my father cutting the wood from their bedroom, and hear Harry kind of growling, right on the brink of snoring himself. I woke up as soon as my mother flicked on the light. In fact, believe it or not, I was awake a second before and saw it come on. Even though it's dark exactly like the night, and even though the room's light is the same light, it's different because you know it's the morning. It felt to me like everything was still asleep and that this little lit-up, busy part was just a dream inside it.

My mother stayed awake with me to make sure I did everything I was supposed to do, but it was a good thing we got everything ready the night before because she was in such a daze that she really wasn't a bit of good. She just walked around like a zombie saying things three times over (like Brush your teeth) and doing things (like wiping off the kitchen table) that made no sense at all.

I carried my cassock and surplice down the steps over my shoulder and, I guess, my mother went back to bed even though when I got downstairs our living room lights were on. The streetlights were still on and nobody was out but me and a man (all I could see was his skinny outline and tell he was carrying a lunch box), so I walked as fast as I could.

When I got to church nobody was there, either, so I looked at the schedule to see who I was supposed to be serving with. When I saw that it was Slicer Reiling, I knew I'd be serving by myself. I got my things on and went upstairs at 6:15. But there were no lights on and no priest to be found. I knew it must be Father Ward's mass. Father Ward is my favorite priest, he's everybody's. He's young and athletic and even stops into B&J's once in a while. He and Harry are buddy-buddy because Harry's on the football team and Father calls him the Little Ginzo because he's short and Italian.

I lit all the candles around the altar that were supposed to be lit and sat back in the sacristy waiting for Father Ward. I started getting nervous because it got to be 6:25 and still no priest. I hated to admit it, but I knew I had to do what the 6:30 mass altar boy always had to do when Father Ward was saying the mass which is go and tap on his window.

If you walk up the rectory porch and lean over the railing you can reach Father Ward's window. That's what I did and tapped. Even though I knew I was doing what I had to do, I couldn't help feeling funny about it for religious reasons and also because I knew that anyone who passed by and saw me would yell. I tapped again a little harder but still didn't hear a peep from inside. I saw Mr. Fix, the school janitor, come whistling through the courtyard and stood still with my arms folded across my surplice like I was birdwatching or something. I tapped the window once more, so hard I was afraid I'd break it, then went hustling down the steps and back into the church.

Not two minutes later, Father Ward came walking in, his shoes still untied, and he blessed me in Latin. He coughed a couple of times, then hung his head over the vestments for so long I didn't know if he had fallen asleep again or if he was maybe crying, but pretty soon he lifted the vestments and blessed them in Latin, too, before putting them on.

Mass finally started at 6:39. As usual with Father Ward's masses it was a real quick one, and just like Harry said, when you serve a mass with Father Ward you better keep track of your responses because if you lose track you can never figure out where you're supposed to be from listening to what he mumbles.

There were only a dozen or so people, all of them women, scattered around the front half of the church which was lit so dim it hardly gave any brightness at all to the stained glass. None of the nuns except Sister Ellen were there as though a bulletin got out that Father Ward was serving the 6:30 and they all decided to wait for a better mass. The mass ended at 6:50 and as far as I knew I hadn't made any mistakes, and Father Ward had made only one. He forgot to consecrate the hosts.

When we got back into the sacristy Father blessed me again and began taking off his vestments. I went back out to the altar to put out the candles and refill the cruets. When I returned to the sacristy Sister Ellen was in there with him. Father Ward was sitting at a table—he had untied his shoelaces again—and sadly sipping a cup of coffee and having a cruller which she must have brought. Sister Ellen was standing over by the counter doing all the things that had to be done after a mass—folding the vestments, putting away the hosts, cleaning the cruets and chalices.

You did very well for serving by yourself, Sister Ellen said as she dried her hands. Yeah, well done, said Father Ward forcing a smile. Thanks, I said. Wait till I get my hands on that Slicer Reiling she said, and I shrugged. Say hello to the Little Ginzo for me, Father Ward said, and I caught Sister Ellen, setting out the vestments for the 7:30, just shake her head and laugh at what he'd said.

Sister Ellen was eyeing me funny as I was getting ready to leave. She walked over to the table where Father Ward was and plopped down across from him making like she was exhausted. Why don't you come over and join us. Have a cruller, she said. I said Sure, maybe I'll have a half, figuring that probably there was something she wanted to talk to me about. But she didn't. The three of us just sat there without saying a word, sister listening to the sparrows outside like she was trying to translate a foreign language. It seemed that there was something we should have been doing or saying but none of us could quite think of what that was.

Catch with My Mother

Tuesday was my birthday. I got a pair of Converse (but they were low whites so I had to exchange them), a football, a globe, and clothes. Not bad. Getting presents still is a lot of fun, and I have a feeling it will always be, but the adding a year part is only okay, not the big wonderful thing it was in the old days.

I came home from the courts early today. I was all excited about getting to play with my new ball and getting to scuff it up but all anybody wanted to do is argue. Must be the full moon. I was going to head right upstairs but to my surprise my mother and Mrs. Simmons were sitting on the steps. It was a nice day for halfway through October. The temperature must have gotten into the sixties during the afternoon, but by five o'clock it had cooled off a lot. There had been lots of lazy white clouds floating around all afternoon, but now the sun was getting low, just peaking above the three-stories on the Central Avenue side, and the clouds had pink bellies and their higher parts, which went up like rocky mountains, had turned a dark winter-gray shade.

My mother and Mrs. Simmons sat there in their sweaters, both of them with their hair pulled back. They were eating from Mrs. Simmons' bag of pistachios and all around their lips and all their fingers and the lap of Mrs. Simmons' dress where she had been putting the shells had turned red. They were talking but not really gabbing. Talking more slow and serious. I figured it wouldn't hurt to stay down for a while.

I knew that if it was anything worth really listening

to my mother wouldn't let me hear, so I had to figure out a way to do it without her or Mrs. Simmons noticing. I started playing catch with myself. I'd start about five yards to their right, then toss the ball high up in the air, run up to it and catch it five yards to their left. Once I caught it, I'd turn back upfield, fake and juke and zig and zag, once in a while throw a lateral to myself, spin, break two more tackles, tuck and then plow my way into the end zone. After one touchdown I'd go right back at it looking for another. I know this sounds pretty easy but I'm not such a good catcher that I didn't miss any, and overall I spent more time crawling under cars than I did zigging and zagging.

As the breeze picked up and kept getting cooler and cooler, they talked softer and softer. Both of them leaned their heads in and down like a pair of birds with their eyes on the same chunk of bread, once in awhile bobbing in agreement. I kept running back and forth, and even though I was spinning real close to them and lateralled to that side every time, I wasn't having much luck picking up any information.

By twenty after five, I had been under the Lobue's Ford four times, under Dick's station wagon three, and over B&J's and into the Pavone's backyard twice. I smelled like a bottle of Seagram's 7 and felt miserable grimy from all the oil puddles I'd crawled through. One time I spun too close and tripped over the bottom step. I waved to my mother and Mrs. Simmons as I flew past and scraped my knee when I landed. My mother said What in the world are you doing, mister. Come over here and take a rest. I said Oh, I was just practicing. There's a game Saturday but a rest might be a good idea.

No sooner did I sit down than Mrs. Simmons got up to leave. I said to my mother So what were you and

Mrs. Simmons talking about. Without blinking an eye she told me. The Simmonses are going to be moving, she said. I said Oh, yeah. She said Yeah, Mr. and Mrs. Simmons, Mr. Simmons especially, are too hurt, they're so hurt, about losing Jeannie. I said And so they want to get away from around here. Yes, exactly, she said. There's too many reminders in the neighborhood. Everywhere they turn. It hurts too, too much.

I felt so sorry for them. Really, Mrs. Simmons didn't look all that bad but Mr. Simmons had really become a wreck. He looked dirty and grubby half the time, and miserable and bewildered all the time. My mother said They're moving because they don't want so many reminders. You can understand that, can't you. And I said Sure, I can understand it. But still something didn't seem kosher to me. She was being too willing and agreeable about the whole thing and there had to be something she was hiding.

By this time the temperature must have been down close to forty. The pink had turned to purple and there was less of it and more of the gray. My mother sat there hunched up with her sweater buttoned to the top. Her arms were crossed and her hands were up inside her sleeves holding her elbows. There she sat, rocking back and forth, smiling a smile that made her mouth tighter instead of wider like a smile normally does.

I said What's so funny. She said Let's play catch. I said you can't catch. She said I can so. She wasn't a good catcher and she was a worse thrower which meant that I spent more time than ever crawling under cars. But mom kept flinging the ball and smiling. Whether she threw it ten feet away or right to me, whether she caught it or watched it sail right past her head, she kept smiling the same smile. She said Go way back so I went way back and she threw the ball clean over a Hoeniker's milk truck. The ball landed in the middle of the street. Just as I got to it, it took one slow tumble then another then another and I had to go crawling again. I just collapsed to my knees shaking my head which she thought was the funniest thing since Barnum and Bailey even though normally she would have been all upset about how dirty I was getting.

The smile was one that meant that she loved me (of course), but it was also a wiseguy smile. A typical mother's smile, like she had known all along about my sneaky little ways and thought they were very cute but futile. As she kept throwing and smiling and cracking herself up, I kept getting more and more suspicious cause she always thinks I'm cutest when she's just gotten one over on me.

White When Pelted

Just like last year, me and Franny and Mo decided ahead of time that we were too old for trick-or-treating then regretted it when the day came, figuring it would have been a good way to pick up an extra couple of dollars. It was after five o'clock with most of the younger kids already on their way home when we finally decided to try our luck even though we had no costumes.

Franny was dead set against the idea at first, saying that we'd be interrupting people right in the middle of their suppers. Mo said trick-or-treating late was the best time because you'd be likely to come across a couple of old ladies who felt guilty about not having any Halloween stuff left to give and would give you a quarter if you were nice about it. He said that he'd ring the bells and that all we had to do was stand there.

To make it look like we had costumes on, we all messed up our hair and tucked our pants into our socks. Franny switched his right and left shoes and walked around with a stick that he called a cane and said he was The Cripple. Mo put his jacket on backwards and made spots on his face with chalk and said he was The Cripple's Leper Brother. I tied my hood on as tight as I could so all you could see was my mouth and nose and barely my eyes, and I tied my belt around my neck and called myself The Hanged Man.

It was a very gray sort of day all day long, and by the time we got started it was getting pretty dark and breezy out. When we turned the corner from Hancock to Congress, Boo jumped from behind some garbage cans and pelted us with a flour sock which is a sock filled with flour and makes you white when pelted. Me and Franny thought that getting whacked like that was pretty funny and added to our costumes, but Mo had a puss on and kept brushing himself off so Boo just kept on pelting him until Mo finally said it was funny. Boo said he'd walk around with us but not trick-or-treat because of his age and that he wouldn't take anything from anybody.

We had been trick-or-treating for almost an hour and we were getting pretty discouraged. All we'd gotten was 30 cents each, a bunch of candy that Mo sold to some little kids for a quarter, and three rotten apples that we immediately threw against the stone wall. We decided to try the apartment building on the corner of Sherman and Congress, and also decided that unless we made at least 50 cents apiece we'd stop. Wake Parish lived in the building and Boo said Wake would be good for a quarter but when we looked at all the bells and mailboxes half the names were missing and we couldn't find any Parishes.

There were five floors in the building and six apartments on every floor. We tried all thirty apartments and all we got for our trouble was ten cents and three home-made brownies that we were afraid to eat. By the time we were done, Franny was really walking like a cripple, and from the chalk and the flour and his own sweat, Mo really did look like a leper with his jacket on backwards, but he still tried to break the deal by saying we should try the twin apartment across Congress. Franny said that Mo was crazy and that his feet were killing him, and Mo came back with You think it's fun to be stuffed in this jacket, and I said How about me and scratched under my hood, and Boo, sitting on the steps, pointed at Franny's feet and laughed at the stupidity of it all.

To try to solve the argument I said that I'd heard that people lived in the cellar and that we could try that. Mo said People don't live in cellars, rats do, but when Boo said it was true everybody believed it. Mo said Alright and Franny didn't say anything but started limping towards the cellar door.

He reached in and found the switch and turned the lights on. When we got down inside, even I found it hard to believe that anybody lived there. It wasn't at all fixed up like some cellars I've seen. It was just a damp stone cellar with bare lightbulbs and clotheslines and ancient baseball bats and stuff and puddles and holes in the cement floor.

We walked ahead and turned left at the third

wooden beam, and the next thing we knew we were in the middle of a kitchen. A mother and three skinny kids, two girls and a baby boy in a high-chair, sat around their table. Since there were no walls, though, this was not only their kitchen but their living room and bedroom, too. There was something very weird and eerie about it--the kitchen table and the couch and the tv and the beds all being in the same area. We stood there looking at them and their round rugs and two little windows up almost to the cellar's ceiling but still barely higher than the ground outside. They looked back at us. We had no good explanation for ourselves.

Mo said Trick-or-treat and all three kids started laughing, including the baby with no teeth who I don't think understood a thing. The mother got up and pulled a big curtain shut and they disappeared except for the giggling. We stood like statues around the curtain, even Boo not knowing what to say. All of a sudden we heard a hoarse kind of mumbling from further ahead. Boo started walking towards it, more because he thought it was his place to do something than because he really wanted to. Franny dragged himself along next. He'd gotten rid of his cane and now was walking more like the Hunchback of Notre Dame than like The Cripple. Mo was third and made sure I stayed right in back of him so no one could jump him from behind. I took the belt off from around my neck and pulled off my hood.

We got to another spot that had a curtain around it and Boo put his ear to it. He pointed to let us know that that's where the noises were coming from. I knew there must have been a good reason why we were still down there, but I couldn't guess what it was.

There was some very creepy moaning and

groaning going on and we could hear the person shuffling around. Then the moaning and moving around sounds stopped and for a full minute there was dead silence. Finally we heard some scrambling back around the door that we came in through and Mo let out this little weep. Boo got up on his tiptoes and started sneaking towards the curtain like he might try to look over it. After a few steps, the voice said Stop. We froze. I want some children for All Hallows' Eve, it said. Then the lights shut out and the voice said, Yes, Franny and Boo, Mo and Monk, I do need some new innocents for my plan.

There we were, surrounded by the voice, maybe by a spirit. We were trembling, our mouths making little noises that we couldn't stop, when all of a sudden a match lit and there was a man's unusually hairy arm holding a crucifix and right behind it was Wake Parish's grinning face. I guess seeing that it was Wake should have made it a little easier for me but it really didn't, just made it a different kind of scary.

Wake started laughing pretty hard because he scared us so much and must have just took it as a harmless joke. He put the lights on and gave us some soda and potato chips—turned out that that area he was creeping us out from was where he lived—and let us watch tv and was very friendly, but we were still kind of leery about the whole thing until Wake said that this had been like an initiation and that from now on we could use his place anytime we wanted to. (Sure, Wake, I said to myself, every day.) Once he said that, though, Boo got a wise look on his face like the whole thing had actually been pretty reasonable and earned his seal of approval. Mo poured himself another soda and got up and changed the channel. I was trying to figure out what I had been initiated into and was still feeling queasy about the tv and the kitchen table and the bed and a lounger chair all being in one room. Franny took off his shoes and leaned back against the couch. Wake rubbed Franny's feet and laughed, very pleased, and I watched all the laughing and I laughed, too, even though I was still trembling.

All Saints and All Souls

After yesterday's to-do with Wake, it was a good thing we had today off from school. I did what I call some real foul-weather thinking. I sat around my room for most of the afternoon, wasting what except for the chill and a little cloudiness would have been a perfectly good day off.

This morning at mass, I saw Cotton Parish having a long, secretive talk with Mr. Simmons, and that got me thinking about all three things--about Wake and how he's acting odder and odder, about Jeannie's death which I think of any time I see any of the Simmonses and some of the time when I don't, and about religion, God, and church, today being All Saints Day (for all the souls in heaven) and tomorrow being All Souls (for all the souls whose whereabouts we don't know).

We're Catholics and we believe that there are six Holy Days of Obligation. Christmas, New Years, the Ascension, the Assumption, All Saints, and the Immaculate Conception. Those are the days of the year, besides Sundays, when it's a mortal sin if you miss mass. A mortal sin is a grievous offense against the will of God. Beside missing mass on a Holy Day of Obligation or any regular Sunday, murder and blasphemy are also mortal sins. Think of your soul as a milk bottle and imagine that as a baby, once Baptism washes away Original Sin, it's perfectly white. A mortal sin blackens the whole thing. All of it. If you die with a Mortal Sin on you before doing penance you go immediately and permanently to hell.

Naturally, who wouldn't want to do penance on earth instead of burning in hell for all that time. This is the reason God created Confession. (Sometimes they call it the Sacrament of Penance and other times they call it Confession. You can call it whatever you want, but the thing to remember is that to be forgiven you can't do just one. You can't just admit to it and say you're sorry, and you can't just do your own penance to make up. You absolutely must do both.)

Confessions happen in the quiet of our church on Monday and Wednesday nights from 6:30-8:30, and Saturday afternoons from 1:00-5:00 even if there's a marriage going on and you and your sinning self have to walk in right in the middle of it. First, you bless yourself with Holy Water, then go into the confessional and kneel down and wait. The priest pulls up the screen which is about a foot wide, and you still can't see him because there's another one there, but a Halloween-orange light sifts through from his room, and a maroon smell comes across with it. Then you know he's got his ear up. You say the Bless me father, for I have sinned, and then you tell all your sins. When you are finished he asks if you are heartily sorry and you say Yes and you say an Act of Contrition while he whispers in Latin and more maroon comes oozing through. Then he gives you your penance and you leave. You go kneel in a pew and say your prayers.

That's it. The whole thing takes no more than ten minutes, penance included.

Now, that's all for venial sins, of course. I've never committed a mortal sin so I can't say how different that penance would be. (Maybe you have to play right field for the rest of your life, haha.) But I do know that mortal sins and venial sins themselves are very different. They are profoundly different because no matter how many apples you have they don't add up to an orange. I'm sure the penance would be a lot more than three Hail Mary's and, using the same thinking as with the apples and oranges, something a lot more hard on you than even saying ten or twenty of them.

But like I was saying to myself a little while ago after a whole afternoon of thinking that started this morning outside church, it seems as clear as a smack in the face that anybody would have to feel a lot better about confessing and doing their penance here, than having their black souls burn for eternity in the fires of hell.

LATE FALL

My Five Season Theory

Like I was trying to explain to Harry, there are two types of seasons. There are regular or Annual Seasons and there are Monk Seasons. As we all know, there are four Annual Seasons—Winter, Spring, Summer, and Fall. But there are five Monk Seasons— Early Fall (from the beginning of school until All Saints Day), Late Fall (from November 2nd, the day after All Saints until Christmas), Winter (from January 2nd or 3rd to Easter Vacation which is usually around the middle of March), Spring (from then until the end of school), and Summer (vacation). You may have also noticed that this leaves room for two of what I call Little Limbos. One Little Limbo is from Labor Day weekend until the first day of school (or actually the first full week of school), and the other is from the day after Christmas until the day we go back to school.

One thing I have to say for Harry is that he was very polite. All the while I was explaining, he kept on smiling and eating his spaghetti. When he was finished eating, I was finished talking and I said See, Harry, I was right. Right. He got up from the table very calmly, put his dishes in the sink, called my mother into the kitchen and put his arm around her. Still very calmly, he pointed with his other hand to his noggin and advised her that she better have me checked.

Sister Ellen and the Other Nuns

Like we do every Friday, we had music class this afternoon. Usually Sister Rita (Little Doom) and Sister Dorothy (Big Doom) teach it. Big Doom is the worst. She's six-foot tall and hits with books, rulers, erasers, and anything else that happens to be handy, even when there's no reason for it. She wasn't there today because one of the fourth grade lay teachers was absent and she took her place. So Sister Rita who is just as old as Sister Dorothy but only about half her size was left on her own. Franny spent the first half of class imitating her and I spent that half hour with my desk top up and down, hiding under it when I couldn't keep from cracking up.

Sometimes Little Doom gets in the habit of saying God be willing every time she mentions something that hasn't happened yet, as though there's a pretty good chance she won't be around when it does. Today she must have set a record. Even the real good kids had a hard time keeping straight faces. But when she said Our Sweet Jesus be willing about a class we were going to have in less than a week and went to cross herself but got her shoulders mixed up between the And-of-the-Son and the And-of-the-Holy-Ghost parts, the whole class had their desk tops up. So then she said God be willing you'll all be here for that class, just to remind us that we could all be hit by lightning or something worse before the week was up. Franny started giggling and snots started coming out of his nose like out of a bubble-maker. He hid his head and wiped it on his cuff. He looked at me, and I knew he was going to do something funny. He itched his neck

under the collar just like Little Doom does and said
Next week I'll be rid of these blasted warts, God be
willing, and he scratched some more. I had to stuff half
my handkerchief down my mouth to keep from
busting out laughing, but when Ninette Greco tickled
me from behind, I did. That's when Sister Ellen came
marching in and said she wanted to see me and Franny
after school.

We met her in a classroom on the third floor. It's
different up there because they hardly use those classes
anymore and it smells very stale. It's really something
how slow time passes when you have to stay after.
When you first get up there and look out the window,
everybody from school is still milling around, but a few
minutes later the streets are like a ghost town. The
same with the hallway. First there's a few kids around
doing chores, then just teachers, then no one. You
look up at the clock and it's still only quarter past three
and you start praying for real.

Sister Ellen sat at the teacher's desk marking
papers. Me and Franny sat at ours staring out the
windows with our hands folded, listening to the echoes
of kids who came back to the schoolyard to play. Sister
Ellen said You know, you shouldn't make fun of Sister
Rita, or of Sister Dorothy, either. She said that they
lived in very different worlds from ours and that now
they were very old and that we should try to
understand not just for their sake but for the sake of
our souls. She asked if we were sorry and we said Yes.
She asked if it was going to happen again and we said
No. Lots of times when they ask you questions like
that it means they're gonna let you go, but this time it
didn't. Instead, Sister Ellen got up and opened the
window. It was November and a lot of yellow-brown
leaves still swung from the trees. You could kind of

smell the season.

At about a quarter to four, she put her papers away and sat at the desk right behind me. At first I didn't turn around because I didn't know what she had in mind, but I did feel pretty uncomfortable with her eyes in my neck. I looked at Franny who shrugged and folded his hands back up. She asked how we were doing in the subjects she didn't teach us. Then she asked Franny how his mother was getting along. Then she said You can turn around, you know. I'm not going to bite, and this relieved me quite a bit. Franny said Better.

She was leaning back in her chair, her crossed legs out in the aisle. The breeze ruffled the bottom of her habit which was almost see-through in the parts where it was just one layer, like a black veil over her legs. She smiled and a bunch of white bubbles appeared in the space between her front teeth making her look like something other than a nun. She said You know, I think Jeannie Simmons was my favorite girl in your grade. There was something so tender about her. Sometimes I actually think I see her, not in school, mostly outside. Franny said he'd thought he'd seen her once, too, standing outside the courts but that it was just his imagination and he shook his head and said something about it being funny how the mind works.

Sister told us about one time when she met Jeannie and her mother up on Central Avenue right before First Communion a couple years back. Jeannie's mom was coughing and sneezing all over the place and they were going to have to leave the avenue without picking out Jeannie's dress. Then, Sister Ellen told us, Jeannie said that I could help her pick one out—and you could see Sister was about to bust out in tears even though she hadn't gotten to any sad part—and her mother thought that was a wonderful idea. So Jeannie and I went into the Globe and she must have tried on every dress she could fit into. I never thought that such a frail girl could contain so much energy. I mean, really, it takes a lot out of you to go back and forth into the dressing room like she did. Sister obviously got a kick out of the whole thing. She told us everything there was to tell. I could really picture the two of them there like a couple of friends, Jeannie going into the dressing room and coming out with the little hump on her back covered in a red with flowers, then a blue plaid, then a solid green, as if she was putting on a new hump each time.

Then, Sister told us, I took Jeannie down to Meyer's for ice-cream. We sat in there for nearly an hour and had such a nice, nice time. It wasn't like I was a nun talking to a young girl, not at all. We just talked very normally, she said, enjoying our ice-cream. I remember being her age. I could have just sat and sat and sat. It was so refreshing, so youthful.

Sister Ellen looked out the window and, as though she could see the breeze coming all the way from the other side of the trees, she moved her eyes from out there to where it fluttered the black habit over her black stockings. I felt something special about Jeannie, a special sort of connection that what she was was what I was fifteen years ago. And that what I was, back then, I'm not that now . . . not just that I'm grown up . . . but . . . oh, well, I guess you don't get it. It's foolish to think about anyway.

Sister was right about that—we didn't get it. Franny and me had been smiling the whole time, not because we thought anything Sister said was funny but just because we were liking her so much.

It was getting late and I didn't have much clue as

to when Sister was going to let us out, and as much as we liked her company it would have been kind of nice to get home, too. From the stairwell, I heard sounds like storm clouds rumbling a long way off, and Sister Ellen said to shut the windows. A few seconds later, the hall door swung open and we could see the Duo of Doom (Sister Rita and Sister Dorothy), and two other nuns who looked like younger versions of those two, come sweeping through the hall.

Sister Ellen said Go home now, it's past 4:30. Go home, go home, hurry up. Oh, go home, boys.

THE COURTS

The courts. The courts. Thank God for the courts.
When you start feeling itchy,
When you start feeling grey, oh yeah,
When you start feeling blue, oh, boy,
Thank God for the courts
And Franny and Slicer and Mo,
Thank God for the courts, oh, yeah,
Thank God for the courts, oh boy.

-Monk

(No applause, just send money.)

B&J's In the Nighttime

It was the night before Thanksgiving and I was watching tv down in the bar with my father, sipping a 7up and eating pretzels, feeling very good about the fact that I had four days off from school coming up.

Things started off like a quiet enough night. The guys seemed a little serious maybe, but I figured that was no business of mine. Joe McGill, an older guy with white hair and pink skin, was tending bar in his usual short-sleeved white shirt. Each year Rheingold Beer holds a Miss Rheingold beauty contest. All the saloons get big cardboard posters with the pictures of six pretty girls on them. You have to fill out a ballot and drop it in a small box attached to the bottom of the poster to vote. Joe McGill really liked Number 4, the redhead with the wink in her eye, and this being the last week of the election, he was sitting down at one end of the bar filling out as many ballots as he could for her.

Two men who didn't come into B&J's very often but were regulars at Thomas J. Maresca Association were sitting at a little wooden table next to the front window. They were brothers, Frank and Gus Pepperini. They were smoking stogies and playing gin and never looked at one another. The only words I heard them say were Gus, gin or Frank, knock. Even the points they didn't say, but just wrote them down on a napkin which they then turned upside down.

Me and my father sat near the middle of the bar, a little closer to the tv end than to the Pepperini end. With the combination of the sweat and grease still in his clothes from work and the soap he used to wash up and the beer and shots he'd been drinking, my father smelled just the way I like him to. Down a few seats from us, nearer the tv were Mr. Caruso and Wake Parish having a very lively but low-voiced conversation which I was doing my best to hear.

Wake seemed awfully serious about the whole thing, just about to break into a sweat. Meanwhile, Mr. Caruso and his pipe were very proud of one another, as usual, and I was convinced that no matter how much he rubbed his head or squeezed his eyebrows together, he was enjoying every minute of it. He was really belting out his d's and t's like there was something especially important about those letters, and you could see his bald head ringing every time he spit one out. Him and Wake were talking about justice and about paying debts. They were talking about mercy. Then they'd start wagging their heads and jump back to justice or maybe sideways to vengeance. But all of it was those kinds of things, like the Baltimore Catechism meets the Twilight Zone.

My father kept trying to get my attention off them and on the tv but had no luck with me until he gave me a quarter to play pool. Even then I was able to listen in pretty much by circling around the table. I was pretending to be trying to figure out the lay of the balls, but I couldn't figure out why my father and Joe McGill were doing their best to pretend like Wake and Mr. Caruso weren't even there.

I was shooting way better than usual and had a run of three balls going until I scratched. I was waiting for the cue ball to come out when Corcoran walked in. Corcoran has a strange head. His chin sticks out farther than his nose. His eyes are real small and set way back in his head where they're always in the dark like two caves cut out from just under the wall of a cliff. All in all, his head looks like a bell that's been split down the middle from top to bottom with the back of Corcoran's head being the sliced side of the bell.

We didn't know Corcoran very well. But we did know that Wake hated him and that he was a trouble maker who got away with things more often than he got caught. We all straightened up a bit when he came in. Corcoran sat down between my empty seat and Mr. Caruso. You could tell by the way he ordered his drink and threw his money down on the bar that he was drunk already. Wake and Mr. Caruso turned in towards one another even more than they had been and kept talking. My father laid his hands on the bar and curled out his lower lip like he always does when he's pretending he's relaxing.

Sitting there, Corcoran would just scowl at Wake and Mr. Caruso and shake his head. Then he'd look around at my father or Joe McGill like he knew something, but when they wouldn't nod back, he'd grin and say something to me and I'd curl my lip out and get ready for my next shot.

Mr. Caruso said It's guilt. Guilt, Wake, and there's no need for it. When Corcoran heard that he let out with a Bullshit, and he did the same thing with his letter t as Mr. Caruso had been doing with his except more so by slamming down his shot glass when he said it. Joe McGill jumped up from his chair and knocked the Rheingold poster over. My father stiffened up. Mr. Caruso stared at the tv and the Pepperini brothers gathered their cards and rose to leave. They both put decks of cards in their sweater pockets, buttoned them, and came over to pay Joe. Gin, said Gus to Joe and Joe said Knock back. Knock, Frank said to Joe and Joe said Gin back and Gus and Frank Pepperini left.

What the fuk are you talking about, said Corcoran to Wake. Mr. Caruso leaned back out of the way. Wake looked at Corcoran in the oddest way. I thought it was like they were both from the planet X37 and Corcoran was talking that language and Wake couldn't figure out how he had gotten here to Jersey City and found him in B&J's. What bullshit are you talking about, asked Corcoran, you stupid mother fukker. You know, my friend, my old friend, you are hiding nothing from nobody. You're scum. Dirt, trash. Then he spun around in his seat and rocked his head in this direction then in the other.

My father told me to get upstairs and he meant it but I didn't go. I made like I was going to but just hid down at the end of the bar past Wake, behind the refrigerator that wasn't plugged in, near the hallway down to the cellar and the staircase up to our apartment.

Finally, Wake managed to get some words out. Shut your god-damned mouth, nobody was talking to you. And Corcoran said Parish, you're a killer. Scum. You're scum. You don't belong among decent people.

My father gulped. Why don't you lighten up, he said to Corcoran. Corcoran laughed and said Fuk you, pal. You'll mind your own god damned business if you know what's healthy for you. My scalp felt electricity running through it and I almost cried and my heart nearly busted with wishing someone had a gun to blow Corcoran's brains out.

Wake was trembling so much when he got up to leave that he couldn't even pick his change up from the bar. Go ahead, go home before I kick your face in, said Corcoran. Wake grabbed one of the cues. He rapped it across the table and broke it in two. He stood there as wild as could be. First he glared at Corcoran like he was a real demon, but then all that drained from him and he stood like he was in a daze. He stared at the stick in his hand like why was he holding it, it was no good to him. Corcoran said Good night, Mary, you better go home now.

Wake jabbed the broken cue into the top of the pool table leaving a long cut in the felt before he disappeared.

Later That Same Night

I let five minutes pass, thumped the steps a few times as though I had just come down, and walked back out to the bar. I asked my father if I could shoot another game of pool and since Corcoran was passed out, head on the bar, he gave me another quarter.

I racked up at the opposite end to avoid the rip Wake had made, and from then on pretended like it was no bother at all, not even there, figuring that complaining was the worst thing I could do.

I was going slow, really taking my time shooting, every now and then walking over and standing in the doorway as though I was looking out for a reason. I'd lean against the door frame with my ankles crossed and the cue held out in my right hand. Sometimes, I'd even take a walk out to the curb and pull up my pants, look up and down the street pretending I was expecting somebody, then spit, tap the fire-alarm box for luck, and return inside.

By ten o'clock, more than half an hour after all the commotion, Corcoran was snoring and Joe McGill was back stuffing Miss Rheingold ballots. My father and

Mr. Caruso, on opposite sides of Corcoran, were watching the Lawman, and you could tell by the way they were finally really paying attention to it that most of the tension had drained out of the place. I don't know about the hard feelings—that's a different story.

I was setting up a corner shot when I lifted my head and saw Cotton Parish standing in the doorway. His eyes were like big marbles. All of a sudden he took two lunging steps and leaped onto Corcoran. His left leg landed on the floor and his right knee, with everything he had, smashed Corcoran's back so hard that after his chest bounced back from the bar something inside him gave a second jerk and he went flying onto the floor. All the noise he made was the one right when Cotton smashed him, a sound like he was choking.

Cotton stomped on his head once and was about to keep it up when my father and Mr. Caruso grabbed him from in front and behind. Me and Joe McGill stood flabbergasted, staring at one another with our mouths open.

Father Ward, who must have been walking past B&J's just then, came hurrying across the floor and knelt over Corcoran. He raised Corcoran's head. First thing he did was open Corcoran's mouth and look in there and stick his fingers in. No blood, he said. He put his ear next to Corcoran's mouth and pulled his eyelids back and Corcoran rolled his head left and right as if to say Where am I. Father nodded his head and asked Joe for a cold, wet rag. He pressed it to Corcoran's face and said some prayers.

In a bit, Corcoran started coming around. Thank you, Father. Thank you, Father, he repeated. With Father Ward's help he got to his feet. I'm okay, Father. I'm okay, he said, pressing his hand to his chest. You want to go home then, Father asked. Yeah, yeah, I'll go home, Corcoran said. But it doesn't change anything. That man's brother is a killer, he said and pointed back at Cotton who was still being held by my father and Mr. Caruso. They were about to let go but it seemed like Cotton didn't have his legs under him so they continued to hold on.

Remember, no matter what anyone says, that man's brother is a killer, Corcoran said as he stumbled out the door where Sister Ellen had been standing all the while. Excuse me, miss. Excuse me, please he said and lunged out past her to the street.

The Card and the Letter

I went down to pick up the mail this morning, today being Saturday, and as expected there was nothing for me. But in the mailbox was the first Christmas card of the season, and I thought it was kind of nice that it came on the first day of December. I dropped all the bills on the kitchen table and walked into my bedroom with the card.

It was from the Simmonses, which I knew from the return address since I hadn't opened the envelope yet because I wasn't sure if I was supposed to or not. Their address was now 122 Hillside Drive in Berwick, Pennsylvania. I put the card down on the bed and tried to picture their house and neighborhood. In my imagination it was very peaceful and happy, their white sidewalk and little lawn like a TV show, but then my imagination went inside their house where it was very quiet and gloomy. I thought of Mr. and Mrs. Simmons sitting there in the living room with their slippers on though it was the middle of day.

The envelope was addressed to Jack and Josie Fillipetti. Since I'm part of the family, I decided I could open the envelope and if my parents yelled that was too bad. It wasn't much of a card—just a 25 cent Hallmark, kind of small, nothing shiny or rough feeling, with a Santa on the roof of the house and the reindeer waiting and one big star in the shape of a crucifix with sharp tips in the royal blue sky. I spun myself around on the bed so I was laying on my back facing the wall with my rear end tucked up against it and my legs going straight up the wall. I opened the card to see if the inside was any better and a folded letter fell out. At its top, the letter said Dear Josie. It was written in ink with lots of scribble-outs, scribbled out so much you couldn't read them even if you tried.

There were really two parts of the letter. There was the first part which said Hello and asked how everybody was doing. It said how much both Mr. and Mrs. Simmons missed Jersey City and their friends and Saint Paul's and the old neighborhood. Mrs. Simmons said she was lost without an A&P and a John's Bargain Store and Havemeyer's—she said she might have to make a trip back to Jersey City just to buy some coffee cake for Roger, who is Mr. Simmons. Then she said how nice Berwick was in its way. Mrs. Simmons used most of the front side for that stuff, and the back side, which was a lot harder to read and the part with all the scribble outs, for real different stuff.

The second part was all about how the Simmonses really felt. Mrs. Simmons said she was doing pretty good, but that Mr. Simmons wasn't, and that this had her worried. He said that what happened last summer, what she called last summer's decision, had had opposite effects on the two of them. That doing what they did brought her peace of mind and that she was sure they had done the right thing. That God would be their only judge. She said she was sure Jeannie was still with them and that she knew Jeannie was happy now.

Mrs. Simmons said she knew it would have been much harder if she had been the one to make the decision. That's why it was so different for Mr. Simmons. See, there were times when she'd sit in the kitchen after supper, after he left the table, and just cry because she felt so bad for him. Since he first approached Wake back in July, she wrote, he hadn't slept a single night straight through. Sometimes he calls himself an idiot and sometimes a coward and sometimes a monster. Sometimes he just sits and drifts away. When she calls he almost never responds and even when he does it's never to what she's actually calling to him about but always to what he's been thinking about all along anyway. What if this and what if that. Why?

Then Mrs. Simmons started a new paragraph.

She said she was sorry for burdening my mother with her troubles because she knew everybody had their own. She asked how I was doing and wished each of us a Merry Christmas, and she said that she hoped to see everybody in the spring but she wasn't sure whether or not that would happen. Not so soon. She signed the card Love, Joycie.

I was still on my back on the bed with my feet up on the wall and stayed like that just a second more after I finished reading. I got right-side up and put the card and the letter back in the envelope. I walked through the hallway to the kitchen. I took the glue from the cabinet under the window and resealed the envelope even though I doubted it would work and knew I didn't have to anyway. I realized that my mother was sitting there at the table watching me do the whole thing so I just handed her the card and left.

The Day I Found Out

Sometimes I think it's only me and a few others, but sometimes I think that nearly everyone knew and that I was the last to find out.

This is the story of the day I learned that Wake Parish killed Jeannie Simmons.

It was the second Saturday of December, a grey day that never gave any hint of where the sun was. We were in the Courts playing tackle football in the snow when Mo came over holding the hand of an adult male Italian. The adult was a little bit shorter than Mo but twice as wide. He was wearing a brown hat with the ear muffs down, a scarf, gloves, and buckled boots up to his knees. The grin on his puss was so wide that when you looked at his face all you saw was his disgusting tongue bobbing around. It was really impossible to notice anything but. He's simple, so don't make fun of him because he's related, said Mo even before we had a chance to and he nodded like he was proud of it. His name was Guy.

After an argument, we had to take Mo on our

side, which meant that me and Mo were on the same team, a pretty sure way to lose a football game. We tried to continue playing but Guy kept getting in the way. Everywhere Mo went, Guy went. If Mo went out for a pass, Guy, slapping himself on the hip as though he was riding a horse, would run right alongside him and try to make the catch too. We told Mo to cover Slicer who was nicknamed Slicer because he ran with his elbows tucked to his side and his arms just moving up and down like he was slicing cold cuts, but every time there was a play, Guy would get in the way causing Slicer to take a sharp slice right at him. One time on an end sweep, Slicer tackled Mo into a big drift of snow near the Bauer's yard. Not two seconds later, Guy came charging over and dive-bombed head first into the snow. His feet started clapping together, and he jumped out of the snow real quick. His face was all red, and he was huffing and puffing for air, shaking his head to get off all the snow, so scared and excited I was afraid he'd have a stroke or something.

We all got a kick out of this and from then on we felt free to imitate Guy and spent more time doing this than we did playing the football game which ended ten minutes later. Me, Slicer, Mo, and Guy were heading over to my house to finish off the afternoon by watching the Little Rascals, but when my mother heard us coming up the steps she locked the door. I'm cleaning, she yelled, you guys are going to have to find another place to hang out. I said Mom, this isn't at all like you, but she didn't answer. Instead, she started singing My Bonnie Lies Over the Ocean just because she knows I hate it so we turned around and headed back downstairs.

Slicer tapped me on the shoulder, looked me straight in the eye and said Either we go down to your basement to make a tent or I'm going home, so that's what we did. There's a stack of five old army blankets in the basement but don't ask me how they got there cause I don't know. If you hang two of them across the clothesline near the furnace and rest boxes on their bottoms to keep them tight against the floor, then light a candle and sit inside you can pretend that you're actually sitting outside in a tent in the wilderness. This is something Slicer loves because he gets to do nothing but make wisecracks the whole time we're in there. His wisecracking voice used to be different from his regular voice but he does it so much that now it seems like that voice is starting to take over his regular voice. Me and Slicer got the tent up pretty good, but we couldn't let Mo help on account of you know who.

We all sat around the candle making jokes and taking turns sticking our fingers in the melted wax until Guy got the brilliant idea that he'd see how close he could come to licking the flame without getting his huge tongue burned off. He started bobbing his head in and away from the candle, hee-hee-heeing all the while. It must have run in the family because Mo, shaking his head and pointing at his uncle, thought it was very funny too. But me and Slicer merely thought it was very, very simple. This will come to no good said Slicer in that serious and wisecracking voice. Trust me, Guy, this will come to no good. And then everybody started laughing the way only Slicer could make you laugh even if you couldn't figure out why what he said was funny. I'm telling you, Guy, this will come to no good, he repeated and we laughed even harder.

Oh, God, I said as things quieted down, and it was then that we realized that we could hear the men in the bar talking right above us. My father was in there. He must have just gotten off from work and stopped in before going upstairs. And Joe McGill was there, and Cotton Parish for the first time in almost three weeks, since the night he almost busted Corcoran in two.

We sat there, listening the best we could. As I couldn't have guessed ahead of time, my father and Cotton were going on about Wake. Cotton said that Wake was getting worse and worse. Real bad. And that he was afraid something awful might happen, and soon. A second passed without anyone talking and I figured my dad must have taken a sip of beer or a drag from his cigarette. Then he said Yeah, I understand, Cotton. I mean of course, sure. I mean I'd do anything. But what, I don't know.

We all stayed quiet and when I looked at the light of the candle bouncing in and out on the ceiling of the tent I realized how spooky it was.

Look, Jack, Cotton said to my father. I'm just telling you how Wake feels. These are his words, not mine. He says he's done something wrong and now has to pay. Understand, Jack. He thinks it's right. He says no man can do what he's done and live with himself. No man, he says said Cotton.

Right then and there I knew exactly what they were talking about, and a chill passed through me from head to toe. Oh God, I thought.

The furnace which was just a few yards away clicked on with a rush, and when it did, my leg jerked out and knocked over the candle. Guy started panting from fear that the whole place, us included, would soon be up in smoke, so he grabbed Mo's bare hand and smacked it down on the flame. Mo yelped and shook his hand to cool it off. Without missing a shake, he gave Guy another good one on top of his head. Slicer got so mad with this fooling around that he twisted Mo's foot in a way that made Mo stretch his whole body out flat to keep it from breaking off.

All the while that this had been going on, I'd been sitting there with my mouth open, too scared to move, because I kept hearing Cotton saying over and over He says killing the girl was murder, he says killing the girl was murder. Each time the words got hammered deeper down into my brain. And every time Cotton got closer to the word Murder, I'd wait, and then finally when I heard it, I'd see it, too. Like on Chiller Theater, a big black M dripping blood, the whole word pulsing like a heartbeat. Killing the girl was murder.

Slicer tapped me and said Where's the match, Monk. Guy and Mo laughed just because it was Slicer who had asked it. I said Did you hear that, Slicer, did you hear what they said. And Slicer said No, I didn't hear a thing, not a word with all the noise these two nitwits were making. You didn't hear it, I asked. No, he said, I didn't hear anything. Where's the matches. I said I don't know, they're on the floor somewhere. We put our hands on the floor and right into the leaky mess that had formed from all the ice and snow melting off of us. Like he had just grabbed the Magic Ring at Palisades Park, Guy raised his hand with the matches in them, but Mo ripped them up right in front of his face because they were soaking wet.

I decided I wouldn't say anything about what I'd heard. I knew there'd be plenty of time for that later, if I wanted to. But for right then, I wanted to be by myself. I said Don't anybody move. Then Slicer made a face and repeated what I'd said and Mo and Guy cracked up. I'll put the light on, I said, so you can all leave.

I got up very carefully and stepped outside the tent. I was real scared. I didn't know what I was scared of exactly except to know that it wasn't any one thing in particular but everything, regardless of what it was in particular. I looked at the furnace and saw it humming away with the red fire inside and that scared me. The stacks of boxes and wood on the table, they scared me. The funny pieces of pipe in my father's little work area, they scared me. Water gurgled down the sewer, that scared me. The sound in Slicer's voice that normally made everything he said funny now made everything he said scary, like sinister. Everything scared me so much that I couldn't even move away from the group. When finally I started walking towards the light switch I went as quick as I could and with a finger on my lips to keep me from eeking. But when I got my hand up on the switch, I hesitated.

I closed my eyes and flipped it but then I was afraid to open my eyes. I gave myself a count of five and then, booof, popped them open. And there was everything, all bright as could be, sitting in front of me. But thank God there was no Wake Parish like I had expected there would be right in the doorway, breathing on me, staring and lighted and wild.

The Ritz Lot

December 14th. Finally, after weeks of stalling, me and Harry convinced my father to get the tree. I'd been passing the Ritz lot all week, watching all the good ones go, but every time I asked him my father would say Tomorrow. And Harry, even though he always wants to be in charge of decorating, is becoming less and less of a help each year as far as going out and buying one is concerned.

Getting ready, my father is so slow you'd think this was the worst torture you could put him through. Or maybe it's me being in a little too much of a hurry. But then when you finally think you've got him all dressed, he sits at the table to rest. He does dress pretty good, though, for someone his age. He doesn't get all bundled in a goofy hat and gloves and ear muffs like some fathers do. He walks with his hands in his pockets and his collar up. Nothing embarrassing. The one thing he does do in the real cold is wear two pair of socks because if there's one thing he hates it's frost-bitten toes. And even though I don't wear two pair any other time of the year, I always do as a tradition when he takes us up the avenue for the tree.

It was very cold out. It must have been in the teens. Everything along Hancock and Sherman and Cambridge was dark like you'd expect it to be. But as we got closer to Central Avenue we could see the people heading back and forth carrying packages, and we could hear them making their soft noises. It was like we were walking right onto a stage. With all the streetlights on, and all the Christmas lights hung across the street, and all the store lights lit, it was almost as bright as day, but yellowish instead of clear.

Even though it was a pain getting my father up the avenue, once he got there he was fine. Turns out he's a real window shopper. First we stopped to look in Havemeyer's. My father fiddled his hands in his pockets and told us about the cookies and candies in tins, about where they came from, Germany or Italy or Belgium, and about which were his favorites and which gave him diarrhea. We made it another half a block then stopped again at Booth's Jewelers where we stood for another good three minutes, my father looking at earrings and brooches, me and Harry arguing about the different kinds of trees, making like we knew what we were talking about. When my father popped a couple of peppermints in his mouth and rubbed the tops of our heads we were on our way again, but before we got to the Ritz lot we stopped every twenty feet to look in the windows of Sandel's Millinery and Grom's Nuts and Enright's Stationers and Cheap Zeke's.

For most of the year, the Ritz lot is just a big lot where there used to be a movie house, but after Thanksgiving they fill it with a hundred or two Christmas trees and string up rows of lightbulbs like a car lot, and they put a sign saying Ritz Christmas Tree Park. By the time we got there, my dad was in a real fine mood. He stared at the first tree right at the entrance then reached his hand out and petted and fluffed its branches. He turned to me and Harry and with a kid's face I'm not used to seeing on him said The Christmas spirit, fellas. Come on, come on, the Christmas spirit.

Walking up and down the aisles of this so-called Christmas Tree Park, all of a sudden my father was Mr. Social. There were fifty or sixty people there, I'd estimate, mostly kids older than me, wearing their high-school jackets—red and white, blue and white, green and gold—or couples alone or with their babies. My father must have winked or smiled at every kid and talked to every adult in the place. He'd all of a sudden just walk up to someone, tap him on the shoulder, and start asking questions. What kind of tree are you looking for? You got your hands full with those boys? Which one of them is your girlfriend? He was worse than my mother and he hadn't even had a drink. I was truthfully a little worried about the way he was acting but Harry said he'd seen it before and it would all pass.

After my father had been doing this master-of-ceremonies routine for half an hour, me and Harry were hoping he'd just pick any tree out so we could get home out of the cold. We'd already seen a dozen that were very nice. But each time one of us would go and mention it to him, he'd say Oh, yeah, that one really is pretty. It may be the prettiest one yet. And then he'd keep right on going, like we'd come to talk and admire and not to buy. So I said You know, dad, we came to buy not to look. Yeah, he said, it is getting kind of cold, isn't it. Me and Harry said Yes. So my father said Yeah. You better go across the street and get me a coffee. We tried to put up a fight and make my father understand we were serious. But the more we complained, the more he laughed—I mean really laughed—until finally he started boxing with us which was a very embarrassing thing for your father to do with all those people around so we gave up and went to get him his coffee at Ginty's.

We got back and hard as it was for us to believe, my father was at it again. He had his left arm around some old man and was trying to pop a Pall Mall out of the pack with his right. The old guy, who was one of the few people there by himself, was a big, husky man with a big brown tweed coat and a hat straight out of the 1940s. He didn't get to say much with my father doing so much yacking. Instead, he looked the ground over, nodding and smiling at what my dad was saying. We gave my dad his coffee and he merrily introduced us. He laid his hands on our shoulders and said Hap, these are my boys. My little guys. Hap's smile spread into a grin and his eyes creased as he looked down at us. Nodding, he put out his hand to shake. My father told us that Hap used to be a terrific baseball player which was hard for us to believe because he was so old and Italian looking. And a shortstop of all things. My father said that him and my Uncle Pat used to go down to Roosevelt Stadium every Monday and Wednesday night for at least three summers to watch Hap play. And Hap said Yeah, you and Patsy must have been about the same size as these guys are now. My father said that one 4th of July Hap hit for the cycle AND hit a second home run in his fifth at bat. My father said he'd never, ever forget it. He said that Dixie Walker gave Hap a tryout with the Dodgers and that he missed sticking by this much and Hap took my father's pretty old hands in his very old ones and spread his palms to show us that this much was really that much.

When it was time to say so long to Hap, my father yelled We'll see you Christmas Eve then, Hap. I've got your word now and you have my address. It'll do you good. Hap disappeared around a row of trees waving as he went—now actually kind of seeming like an old athlete. Harry reached up to poke my father on the head. Hey, Dad, I didn't know we were having a Christmas party, he said. My father poked him right back and said Oh, no, well, dear me. Dear me, you didn't know, and neither did your mother. Oh, Jesus.

We did one more turn up and down the aisles.

Most of the people had left by now and all but two rows of lightbulbs were turned off. When my father threw away his coffee cup, I got the feeling that we were finally ready to leave. I said There, dad, there's a great one. He looked at it and turned out his lower lip to think. Then as though we had just walked into the lot a minute earlier, he says Charity, do unto others, fellas. You know, the Christmas spirit, the Christmas spirit. Well, me and Harry just shook out heads.

We walked back to the main entrance and he picked out the first tree he'd fluffed when we got there. I yelled No, dad, what are you doing. For crying out loud, don't pick that one. Yeah, I know, I know, he said and picked up the tree and paid for it and had them tie it. He tucked it under his arm. He did some kind of little hop-skip then stopped and put the tree down as we looked blocks and blocks up the lit-up avenue. He held the tree at arm's length to get a good look at it, then he doubled over from cracking up so hard. Still laughing, he wiped his eyes and said Oh, goodness. Oh, goodness, wait till your mother gets a hold of this one. This is gonna be something.

We left and as we walked back along the avenue taking turns carrying the tree, weaving in and out of one another, I watched him all the way.

Where I've Always Lived

Down on the ground floor, you can get to the hall steps by walking through B&J's, or you can avoid the bar by coming in through the Cambridge entrance. You climb the stairs and when you get to the top of the stairs, you have to make a left and walk down the hallway about five steps to the door of our apartment. In the hall there are boots, raincoats, umbrellas, baseball gloves, and anything we might be moving in or out of the apartment.

There are four rooms inside our apartment, five if you count the bathroom. The first room you step into is the living room which is something my mother hates. The living room is at the front of the building above the main entrance to B&J's, overlooking South Street, right across from the Courts. To the right of the living room if you have just stepped in and are facing Cambridge Avenue, is the archway to the two bedrooms. First mine and Harry's, then my mother's and father's. There are two windows in our bedroom and there are four in my parents'—two overlooking Cambridge and two over the garage. Standing in my parents' room and facing the back of the house, off to the right is the kitchen which has one window over the garage and through the kitchen is the bathroom. For some reason, my mother likes to say Everything in this apartment is backwards.

Even though the rooms don't look too different from usual, somehow the house really changes around Christmas. The bathroom's pretty much the same though there may be new towels in there and it smells a little more of C.N. or Lestoil. (I'll take Lestoil any day.) The kitchen's nothing special. The refrigerator's full the whole month and there's always a Christmas-colored plastic tablecloth on the table with a shiny bowl of plastic fruit in the middle which I tell my mother looks more like Thanksgiving than Christmas but does look very nice as long as she keeps dusting it which whenever I mention she says You dust it. Then there's my parents' bedroom. The three things that get added to it are new curtains, a new bedspread, and Christmas bells hanging from the crucifix. My room and Harry's doesn't get too changed. This year I nailed a wreath up over my bed and I keep a little reindeer my parents gave me when I was a baby hidden under the mattress but nobody knows about it. And by the week before Christmas the closet is very hard to shut because it's where everybody puts all their wrapped presents which keep building and building almost every day so you have to be real patient and not slam the door otherwise you crush all the boxes like Harry did last year.

The living room is the one that gets the most changed. It's really something. I have to give both my mom and dad a lot of credit for that.

The tree changes the whole room. The tree changes everything. It gets set up on an end table and put right in front of the three windows at the front of the house. In the windows go three sets of electric lights which are almost impossible to plug in without knocking over the tree. Under the tree goes a blanket of white cotton with the manger on top of it. The couch stays where it is, along the wall on the Cambridge Avenue side, and instead of no one wanting to sit on it everybody does. The TV which is normally where the tree is gets moved over next to the hall door and a log with real candles (though they're never lit) goes on top of it. One chair goes next to the couch, half blocking up the archway to the bedroom. The other chair stays where it is, between the TV and the tree. Also between the TV and the tree is the victrola with one or two boxes of candy on top of it. There's a big mirror over the couch with shelves for knickknacks which mostly get taken down and replaced by Christmas ones. Cards get hung all around its edge, and cards also get hung around the archway. They usually get filled up pretty good. This year we're a little behind where we were this time last year.

I love the room like this, I love it so much, especially at night when the only lights on are the Christmas lights. Sometimes all I do is sit there and put Christmas carols on. I shut the light and whisper made-up stuff to myself. That the tree is in a very cold and snowy forest, and that the lights hung around the tree are fruit and that they're glowing because they're giving out warmth. I say the cotton the manger's on is part snow but also part cloud, too. I say the music's coming from my head going out into the room, not the other way around. And I know that that's true. I say cards, candle, gifts, Jesus, tinsel, angels, and bells. Sometimes I say the words real fast and sometimes I say them real slow. I say the names of my friends and of my aunts and uncles, and the names of the guys in the tavern and the people on the avenue. I describe their clothes and faces and the way they walk and I hear them talking. I say the names of the stores and the names of the streets all around our neighborhood. I think as hard as I can of every little thing around me. The slippers my father wears, the things that have always been in the bottom drawers, the way my mother and father look when they fall asleep in their chairs. I think of every bottle in the medicine chest and every pot under the sink so hard I can feel their dents. I think of the smell of B&J's coming up from the hall, the smell of wet towels hung over the radiators, the smell of mothballs and stockings and hat boxes. I sit there and sit there and sit there with the music just flying out of my head.

Falling Asleep by the Window

Today was a really cold day. Twenty-one for a high. I made myself my hot chocolate and pulled one of the living room chairs over by the window so I could relax and warm up but still see into the Courts to know when it was near time that there were enough guys to start choosing.

As I was sitting there watching and drinking, I started to feel very drowsy. It was nice smelling the mixture of chocolate with the Christmas pine and nice feeling the cold drift away from me. I pulled my feet up onto the chair and threw my sweatshirt over myself.

I guess I dozed off for a few minutes because when I looked out and across the street there were five guys in the courts playing catch. I figured I still had some time since we didn't start playing until we had twelve and wouldn't start choosing until we had ten, but I also figured I better keep my eyes open anyway. I curled up again and leaned my head against the window and put my hood on to protect my ears from the surprisingly cold glass. I was watching my breath make circles on the window when I noticed a man walking up South Street, still on the Sherman side of Hancock. I knew it was a man because of logic. It definitely wasn't a woman and I couldn't think of anything else it might be but really I couldn't make much of anything out under all its dark clothes at that distance. I couldn't see any legs moving and I couldn't see any face, just a black blur creeping its way up the street. As the figure got closer I could see something moving up and down off to its left side. The figure was shuffling his feet instead of lifting them and his tipped walk started to look familiar. He rocked his body side to side with each step, like he had no joints—as if everything was molded together in one piece, almost like a beetle.

When he got to the corner of South and Hancock, I realized it was Corcoran. He was all bundled up inside his black leather jacket. I could practically smell the stale cigarette odor it carried. He had a black hat pulled down tight over his head, the right side a little higher than the left (just like his shoulders), a small red feather stuck in the band. His pants were black and his shoes were black, too. As he got closer, right across the street passing the second entrance to the Courts, I could make out what it was that I saw moving off to his left side. His left hand was out and he was bopping it and snapping his fingers.

I must have dozed off again because when I looked into the Courts there were eight guys there. In other words, three more than five. Corcoran disappeared from sight and I just leaned my head against the window again. It was getting harder and harder to get my eyeballs to do what I wanted them to. They drifted down to where I was looking at my own sidewalk and there was Wake. He must have stepped out from B&J's. He pulled his cigarettes out of his pocket, lit one, and squeezed the match between his fingers like it didn't burn at all. In a few seconds he started following Corcoran up towards Central Avenue, even walking the same way as he walked, shoulders slowly rocking, fingers coolly snapping.

I was half asleep and half awake when I heard a peck-peck against the window but the half asleep side won out and I didn't do anything except listen for another peck. Another one came and I opened my left eye just in time to see a pebble coming right at me. I jumped down and there was Franny and Nehru in the street waving to me, yelling that the game was ready to start and I better get moving if I expected to be choosed in.

I was in a real daze and if I hadn't been on such a hot streak the past week I would have just stayed where I was. It took me a couple of minutes to get the right clothes on and to get outside. I crossed and stood at the entrance to the Courts feeling the wind cut through me.

When I heard someone coming up from behind I looked over my shoulder and there was Cotton Parish, huffing and puffing, running faster than usual in the direction of Corcoran and Wake. He didn't even notice me or at least that's how it seemed but when I saw him running like that at least that I hadn't dreamed the whole thing.

An Unexpected Guest

At about 7:30 tonight Cotton came over the house to talk to my father. His hair was as bouncy as ever even though he must have just gotten a hair-cut, but his eyes were more businesslike, colder than usual, and his head didn't bob around so much.

My mother did her best to keep me and Harry out of their way. She said we couldn't listen to Christmas carols, not even *Christmas with the Chipmunks*, because that would disturb them. She said it might be better if me and Harry watched the little TV in their bedroom because they were going to be in the living room. Her strategy worked pretty good, but every once in a while we'd wind up in there anyway, stay for a couple of minutes then leave, but always return again not so much later. Finally, my mother got the very good idea of having us wrap gifts, which she knew we couldn't resist, and this did keep us in the bedroom for just about the whole time. But it didn't keep us from knowing what was going on between my father and Cotton.

I don't know what's going to happen, said Cotton, but I'm scared for him. Last night he was up all night. It's all he ever talks about. Religion stuff all the time. He says he's got to be punished. He says that's what he needs, that it will help him. I don't know, Jack, he's so twisted up. He went to confession but he says he knows God won't forgive him.

Just in case my mother walked in, me and Harry kept cutting the wrapping paper. We listened to every word Cotton said, though, and kept nodding back and forth at one another to make sure we were hearing the same thing. He says he can still feel the sin inside him, said Cotton. He says he tastes it every god damned time he swallows. Atonement and punishment, that's what he talks about over and over. Atonement and punishment. He says he's got to make up, do something good. That's what he needs.

Naturally, me and Harry weren't doing such a good job of cutting the paper. We were approximately 80% listening to Cotton and 20% trying not to waste a lot wrapping paper like we did last year. We wanted to cut the sheets just the right size but instead we kept cutting them too small. So far we'd cut four pieces for the same box but none of them had quite made it and you don't want to hand anybody a Christmas present where a strip of that grey cardboard is showing through all the colorful wrapping. It goes to show what can happen when you think too much and not enough.

When the doorbell rang, me and Harry ran to answer it. It was Wake. He was already inside the hall, standing on the second step. We stood there gawking at him and he said Well, are you going to invite me in or what. We said Sure, come on up, Wake. I yelled Wake's here. He went inside and sat with Cotton and my father.

My father asked him if he wanted a drink and Wake smiled and said Sure do, partner, if you'll be so kind as to pour me one. And for the rest of the time they sat there which must have been about an hour, everything Wake said he said like he'd just walked out of a western—The Rebel, or Palladin, or Lawman. I'm not sure why Wake was doing that, but I'm pretty sure it meant he had everything under control and not to worry.

And it was the best I'd seen Wake look in a long time. He was clean shaven and his hair was slicked back. His whole face was almost polished-looking. He had a very bulky sort of blue sweater on, a pair of green chinos with a good crease in them, and a pair of nice black shoes. Somehow he reminded me of a very eager little boy.

Even the cuts right under his eyes, though they were extremely weird at first, were perfect the way the rest of him was perfect. The cut under the right eye was the older one, maybe a week old. It looked like it was made with a very sharp knife or a razor blade. The cut was right across the cheekbone, and the skin was hard and shiny and stretched tight over the slit. The cut under his left eye was still fresh. It was mostly covered with a clean bandaid. That whole eye was puffed. His eyelids had some mix of black and blue and dark yellow in them, and little bruises of red and blue ran down from the corner of his left eye to the cut.

The Complete Christmas Eve Party

Last night was Christmas Eve and did we have a party. There were ten people there, eleven counting me. The people were my mother, my father, Harry, Hap, Mr. and Mrs. Caruso (Mo was at his cousins' in Greenville), Sister Ellen, Father Ward, and for a little while Wake and Cotton which made me the only kid since Mr. Thirteen Year Old, Harry, was dressed like an adult and kept waiting for his chance to get out and go to midnight mass.

Of all the people who came, it was Father Ward who made the grandest entrance. When him and Sister

Ellen walked in, Father Ward was carrying his black pants rolled up in his hand because him and Sister had just been to an orphanage where Father Ward played Santa Claus. He had taken the rest of his costume off and put his black back on, but hadn't found a place where he could change out of his red pants.

When my father first invited Wake and Cotton, Cotton said he didn't think they'd be able to come. But then, he said, some of their plans fell through so they were able to make it over even though they only stayed for about an hour.

It was during this time, while Wake and Cotton were still there, that Hap told his story about a boy and his monkey. It was an old holiday story, my father told us, and it was some amazing thing.

Hap was sitting at the end of the couch furthest away from the tree. Next to him was Mrs. Caruso, next to her was Mr. Caruso, and squeezed in at the end was my mother. Father Ward and Sister Ellen were sitting in a chair that me and Harry had brought up from the cellar and was barely big enough for the two of them to squeeze onto. My father was sitting in his chair and there was one chair left. Me and Harry had been fighting over this chair the whole early part of the night until the Parishes came over and we had to sit on the floor which I didn't mind but Harry did a lot which made it all the more worthwhile. Wake and Cotton shared the seat but they couldn't fit on it if they sat regular but had to sit back to back like their rear-ends were Siamese twins.

Wake had been putting away the drinks pretty good and seemed very comfortable and relaxed. Mrs. Caruso, who is not very fat but who is all fat, including legs and neck and shoulders, and was sitting next to Hap couldn't keep from tipping and leaning hands first against him even though he must have been fifteen years older. Mr. Caruso just sat there with his legs crossed and puffing on his pipe like he could care less. Cotton and Wake were watching. They were dressed alike in sweaters and chinos, and both of them looked uneasy, but Cotton in a high and talky way, and Wake in a very quiet way. Wake had on the same nice clothes he had on when he came over a few nights earlier except he looked like he hadn't even been out of them since. The cut under one eye had totally closed and now was just a shiny lump. He had taken the bandage off the other one, but it looked like he hadn't really been cleaning it good because inside the slit you could see yellow puss and little grains of black dirt.

Ever since my father had mentioned this story of Hap's, Mrs. Caruso had been badgering him to tell it. Finally, after listening to her for twenty minutes, Mr. Caruso raised up in his seat and said Hap, just tell the story, hah. Would you just tell the story, please. So Hap started telling it and this is my version which I will call Basil and the Stone. Hap got very old-country looking. He leaned back into the cushions like he was leaning back into the time he'd first heard it as a boy. He told the story in groups of sentences that moved up and down like hills.

It's the story of a boy who grew up in Jersey City not so, so long ago. He was the son of a man who had never been to school, not even to first grade, not even for a day. The man, this boy's father, travelled around the city with Basil, the Monkey, making his living as an organ grinder. When working, the father hardly ever spoke—an odd thing for an organ grinder. But instead, he would walk slowly and smile and doff his hat.

Basil and the boy were terrific friends. Never was there jealously or misunderstanding between them. They communicated through their eyes and through the sounds of the bells. This little boy who was the son of an organ grinder and whose best friend was Basil the Monkey, was also the son of a blind woman. In those old days, the young children of blind mothers wore little round bells tied to them.

One bell was always tied to each of the boy's wrists, one to each shoe, one to his belt buckle, and one tied to the cap or hood he always wore. Each bell had a slightly different tone. By listening to the bells the mother knew where the boy was and what he was doing.

When the child reached the age that the bells had to be removed, it was very hard for the whole family. It was the mother's responsibility to decide the right time, knowing that if the bells remained on too long the child could become one of what they called the Odd Ones.

Well, the boy's mother had already allowed the bells to remain on for a long time, too long she feared. She loved the boy so much, and it seemed to her that the bells should belong to him forever, but she knew that the time was coming when she would have no choice.

One day, the entire family, all four of them, were at the docks. Petey the Boy and his mother had come to watch the father and Basil at work, and though the mother could not actually watch, she claimed she could feel a lot of what was going on through her skin. This was Petey's favorite place. In those days, the docks were also the marketplace. They were jammed with people and wooden boxes, open crates not only of fruits and vegetables and cheeses and fish, but of mirrors and linens and dishes and umbrellas and religious things like rosary beads and scapulars, all from Europe. The mother sat knitting as the father and monkey attracted their crowd—the father grinding away at the organ and Basil scampering about, collecting the pennies and nickels and tipping his cap.

A trio of parish nuns, out on a shopping stroll, approached and greeted Petey's mother. She talked with the Mother Superior about poverty, family, and novena and other things a poor woman would talk to a Mother Superior about. Suddenly, in the middle of a sentence, the mother noticed an absence and realized that she could not hear her son's bells. She yelled to him. He left the fruit-wagon pony he had been petting and ran back to her from across the street.

That's when the mother knew it was time to remove the bells. Her husband, sensing what was about to happen, ended the entertainment and came near with Basil. The nuns took a step back, into the second row of the crowd. Tears fell from Petey's mother's eyes as she unknotted the leather strings then held the six bells in her hands.

The boy kicked his arms and legs in silence, and confused (but not as confused as Basil), he and the monkey stared into one another's eyes.

The mother reached for and took the Mother Superior's hands. She placed the bells in them. The nun tucked her hand through a slit in the side of her habit and when she removed it, the bells were gone. The three nuns blessed Petey's mother and hurriedly walked away.

Who knows what went through Basil's mind. Fear. Confusion. A sense of loyalty and love for the boy. He watched Petey and listened for the sounds that never came. The monkey looked at the nuns. He ripped the leash from the father's hands, ran after the nuns, and grabbed back the bells. In doing this, he tore the Mother Superior's habit and cut a gash in her thigh. A sin had been committed and now a stain marked the family.

Basil would have to be killed, but the mother and father couldn't tell the boy what they would have to do.

The next day, just as he would any Sunday, the father brought Basil to the docks. Though the crowd was always smaller on a Sunday, Basil, still thinking he had done a heroic act, was even more gay and spirited than usual. But the father knew what he must do. He brought the monkey to a far and desolate end of the pier. He took a piece of twine from his pocket. To one end, he tied the monkey's leg, to another a large stone, large anough that he had trouble lifting it. He picked up Basil, petted and kissed him. He placed him down at the edge of the dock, and in one great shove pushed Basil and the stone into the bay.

When the father returned home for supper, he told Petey that Basil had run away. For hours the boy sat in a chair in the corner of the living room, his eyes shut and his arms and legs crossed, seeming like he would never move again. That night when he went to bed, Petey dreamed in bells, and in the early morning he woke sure that he could find Basil.

When his mother and father got out of bed, Petey was gone. Gone forever from that quiet house were Basil, Petey, and the bells.

Somewhere in the telling of the story, Hap's eyes shut and even when he finished the story and got his eyes opened, it took him a few more seconds to get each eye lined up with the other. Then my mother, Sister Ellen, and Mrs. Caruso ooo-ed and aah-ed, and the men, even Wake, smiled and Harry applauded like he had just seen a play. I felt so bad for everybody in the story that I could feel the tears ready to overflow down my face.

Well, by that time it was almost eleven. Mrs. Caruso started quiet, but it didn't take her long to be yucking it up again with Hap, and Mr. Caruso was still sucking on his pipe except now he had his eyes closed half the time. My father tried asking him something about the NFL Championship next week between the Philadelphia Eagles and the Green Bay Packers. But Mr. Caruso just shook his head and said Nah, Jack. Nah, nah.

Cotton and Wake were having what seemed to me to be a nice conversation about Christmases past and it made me feel good to see them together like that, especially since Cotton was working so hard at giving Wake a good time. But after not very long, I could tell that Wake's mind was somewhere else and that he was ready to leave. Half the time that they were talking, he had that little boy gleam in his eye, but the other half he had a very tragic look like he'd just seen that boy with the gleam shot and killed. And then that got me thinking about the way he looked the night in the bar with Corcoran and then that just messed me up more because all it did was get me thinking about what he'd been living with all these months.

Cotton stood up and said Well, gentlemen, I think the Eagles will fly, which not only meant that he thought the Eagles were going to win the championship but was a way of saying that him and Wake were going to leave. Cotton said they were going over to see their mother before she went to sleep. That she was all alone and that they had some gifts for her. Cotton tucked his hair under a blue knit cap, and Wake nodded and folded his arms. As they were leaving Wake said Yeah, everybody, we're gonna go over and visit with our mother, and those may have been the only words he said all night that he seemed like he was really willing to let everybody hear.

After the Parishes had gone, I started paying a lot more attention to Sister Ellen and Father Ward. They had been kind of hushed all night, sitting comfortably sipping away at their brandies. When Sister Ellen got up to go to the bathroom she put her very white and bony hand on Father's knee for a boost.

While she was gone, I had to go into the kitchen for more ice. On the way through my parents' bedroom, I heard someone whisper my name. It was Harry. Don't put on a light, he said. Come over here, I'm by the garage window. I went over and sat next to him, the two of us on the window sill. I said Harry, what are you doing in here in the dark, and he passed a tall glass in front of my nose with stuff in it that smelled like peppermint. Schnapps, he said. This is the very best stuff to drink, especially around the holidays. As if you would know, I thought, but didn't say because I didn't want to get knocked through the window. I said Why don't we sit on the bed but Harry said no we couldn't because if we did we'd slop it and then our mother would know somebody had been messing around in there and get suspicious. He said Here, have some. So I took the glass and downed a little. He said Take some more, so I did. I said How much of this stuff do you have, and he said In my drawer. In my drawer I have another pint. I said Boy, Harry, you're just like a real wino, and he said Yeah, I know. He said This is my kind of drink and took another big gulp. The smoothest stuff you can get. Yeah, sure, I said, as if you would know, and I took off for the kitchen, still feeling the warm mint all the way down to my belly button.

I may have been a little drunk.

I stood in the doorway to the kitchen and stared at the closed bathroom door knowing that Sister Ellen was in there and I started thinking and picturing. As an example, when she went to the bathroom, did she pull the stuff up around her waist and hold it in her arms, or did she just let it all drop down around her ankles or was it a complicated combination of both. As another for instance, were her underwear black. I guessed yes. I decided that her legs were white-white and smooth like hair had never grown on them. I wondered if she bounced her knees together and I wondered what she was thinking about while she was in there. For an example, did she think about something silly someone had just said in the other room or did she knock off a decade of the rosary. I wonder if she ever thought about all the stuff she had to lift up or pull down and if she ever regretted anything. As I said, I think I was a little drunk.

When I got back into the living room, Harry was sitting in the chair that the Parishes had left. He really looked drunk and sloppy which was funny because he wanted so bad to look grownup and this was probably the most grownup-looking I had ever seen him. I gave him a healthy smack on the back and he gave me a dirty look with one side of his face. Almost time to leave for midnight mass, I said. Shut up, Monk, he said. I said Hmm, it sure smells pepper-minty in here and cracked myself up.

Then I looked over at the couch and what I saw there cracked me up so much it crippled me with stomach pain. There was Mr. Caruso, his pipe hanging out of his mouth like it was a lead weight. His elbow was on the armrest and his head leaned against his hand, so bored that it looked like his whole face was melting. And there was Mrs. Caruso in the middle of the couch talking away and flapping her wings like a butterfly, pouring brandy down her pipe like there was no tomorrow. And down in the far corner was poor Hap trying so hard to sit up and pay attention that he looked like he had a harpoon in his back, which may not seem too funny now but seemed very funny then.

Father Ward and my father were having a good time talking about Archbishop Baldoni who was staying at the rectory for a month. They were both very good laughers in their way. When he thought something was funny, Father Ward would put his two hands up in front of his face and when he finished would rub his eyes with them. My father's laugh was just a crooked smile with one tooth hanging out from it with an occasional Isn't that something, isn't that something thrown in.

Harry looked like he was coming around a little, or at least trying to. Just to liven things up a little bit, I said So how's everything, Mr. Caruso, but before he could unstick his face from his hand my father told me to go out to the kitchen to see what my mother and Sister Ellen were up to and to bring in two more shot glasses.

Those two came in as I was going out, and when I returned I handed my father the two extra glasses. He said that we were going to have a Christmas toast and that me and Harry could have a drink, too. I thought this was pretty funny. He grabbed hold of a bottle of brandy and poured everybody a shot. Oh, it tasted awful, and little spritzes of it started dribbling out from the corner of Harry's mouth.

This must have been the drink that woke my father up because all of a sudden, when everybody was looking like they were just about to pass out, he got awfully perky. We're going to play charades. That's what we're going to do. It's eleven o'clock said my mother, but he just ignored her. Nobody else seemed all that excited by the idea, either, but everyone went along with it because they all liked my father and it was unusual to see him this pepped up. What should the teams be, he asked. How's about Father Ward, Sister, Mr. and Mrs. Caruso, and Monk on one team. Hap and Harry and Josie and me on the other. Since nobody really cared, nobody disagreed, but I do think that Mr. Caruso was glad that Hap and Mrs. Caruso were split up.

I was the first one to go. The way we play is that the other team whispers the name of a song or a movie or a book to you and you have to try to get your team to guess it without using words. You get up to three minutes (which can be a very long time) and each person on the team takes a turn. When everybody's had their chance, you add up all the times and the team with the least seconds wins.

Like I said, I was the first to go and I got Gone with the Wind. I made a fist and spun it around off to the side of my head and made like I was turning a motion picture camera and they all said Movie. The word Gone is a hard one. I tried waving goodbye and then I tried just leaving the room. I tried doing words that sounded like Gone like Done and Song but all that did was confuse them more. Then I skipped to the fourth word Wind. I acted like I was getting blown around by it and put my hands up around my mouth and started Hoohooing. Harry protested that I broke the rules by making a noise, but it was too late and nobody cared about his protest. Done in two minutes and ten seconds.

The next to go, the first one on the other team, was Hap. We gave him The Scarlet Letter because I just saw the movie on TV the day before. Hap scratched his head like he had never heard of it. When he stood up, he pretended that he had a hat on that he took off. After half a minute it was clear he wasn't going to have much luck since he spent more time scratching and shrugging than he did giving clues. Father Ward and Sister Ellen got up and walked out towards the kitchen. Mrs. Caruso, who was on our team, not Hap's, and already knew the answer, started trying to help him out. While he was trying to find something in the room that they'd call Scarlet, she was kneeling in front of them trying to get the word Letter. This got on Mr. Caruso's nerves and he started making jokes, most of them about his wife's rear end which was sticking in our faces and looked even bigger up close and in purple. They still weren't going to get it, though. My mother and father kept looking at one another, giggling and hugging, and kept saying a hundred times Pen, even though Mrs. Caruso had told them right out loud that that wasn't it. Harry was concentrating on Hap and whatever red thing Hap would point to Harry would say either A Christmas Carol or Moby Dick because he knew I picked the title and he knew those were my favorite Christmastime movies. But him and Hap were getting nowhere fast. Watching Harry guess Moby Dick for whatever Hap pointed at was pretty funny but not funny enough to keep me from having to pee.

Father and Sister were in my parents' bedroom. They were hugging so tight I thought they'd go right through one another. Father Ward had one hand around what must have been Sister Ellen's waist and his other hand was up in her hair. The hat part of her habit was off, laying on the bed. Her hair was almost like I thought it would be. It was light brown and very straight but it was a little bit longer than I expected. She had Father around the chest in a literal bear hug. They were kissing with their mouths wide open and clamped together. Sister Ellen was making little noises but I don't know where from because I don't know how any sound could have slipped out of her mouth. Father Ward did look like a bear from behind with his chest full and the muscles in his neck bulging and his black hair shining.

I don't know how, if it was something they had learned somewhere somehow or if it was automatic or what, but they sure looked like they knew what they were doing. I watched them for a few seconds before I quietly turned around and came back into the living room because I forgot about going to pee which was why I got up in the first place. What I saw hadn't made me squirmy at all. In a way, I actually liked what I saw and wouldn't have minded staying there a little longer.

I got back inside just as Mrs. Caruso was saying the word Letter while she was acting like she was scribbling. Then my mother and father, knowing that the second word was Letter, looked at poor Hap standing there shoving Father's red Santa hat at them and my Mother yelled The Scarlet Letter just before the three minutes were up. Mr. Caruso was fuming that they got it in time and called Sister Ellen and Father Ward back in as though they were about to go into battle together. Sister Ellen came in all flushed and with her habit back on, tipped to one side just like her arch enemy Boo McCann wears a baseball cap.

It was Father Ward's turn and he got a Christmas song. Surprisingly, he was a very good charades player. Maybe it was popular back in his seminary days. The first thing he did was put his finger to his eye and I said eye and he nodded yes. Then he took the logs off from on top of the TV and laid them on the floor. He made a fist over them and moved it back and forth like he was cutting them and I said Saw and he nodded yes again. Before he got to the next word, Harry, who was looking very odd—like he was holding a little bird or something tight in his mouth—got up and left. Father Ward got back to work. He pointed to me then he pointed to my mother, back and forth, until finally we got the word Mommy. Just then a freezing cold breeze came gushing through the room. Father started to pucker like a kiss and I yelled out I Saw Mommy Kissing Santa Claus as my mother jumped up and headed for the bedroom. Mr. Caruso's head started shining for the first time all night and the smoke from his pipe was doing a jig in the air. He wrapped me in a hug as though I had just won him a bouquet of hundred dollar bills.

Uh-oh, then I heard my mother giving it to Harry pretty good even though she was trying to keep her voice down. I went in there to see what was going on. Harry was standing hunched at the window with his head still hanging out. She turned him around and had her finger right up in his face. Harry pleaded innocent to the whole thing—being drunk, messing the bed, ripping the spread, and puking out the window—which was a sad sight to see coming from someone usually so good at wiggling his way out of things. No, she said, and who do you suppose did it then, Sant-y Clause. That was pretty funny, I thought.

When she left it was just me and him sitting on

the bed and he looked like a mix of a lot of things you wouldn't want to be—embarrassed, sick, drunk, disgusted. He pointed to the bed where the spread and the blankets were a mess and where the little rip was and he said There's no justice. I get yelled at for something I didn't even do. I don't know who done that to the bed. I said I'll get you some water then, come on, we'll go back inside. He sat on the edge of the bed still straightening the spread, still repeating I didn't even do this. I put my arm around his shoulder and said C'mon, Harry, I'm your brother. I love you. Let's go back inside.

LITTLE LIMBO

December 25th

Even though today's Christmas Day and it's supposed to be the last day of Late Fall, it felt more like the first day of Little Limbo than anything else. I got up very early this morning even though I didn't get to bed until one o'clock last night. It was still mostly dark out when I opened my eyes for the first time. The window shades were that wet, grey-blue color between morning and night, but I could tell right away that there was no way I could fall back to sleep. I rolled out of bed and checked the clock. It said six o'clock on the button. I put on a pair of socks and sat at my desk to write about last night. I bent the lamp as low as it would bend and was very quiet, trying not to wake Harry because I was sure that if I did . . . well, it wouldn't be a good thing. As far as that goes, though, I don't think I had much to worry about because Harry was snoring to beat the band. It could have been the peppermint schnapps working on him or it could have been my own imagination working on me, but I would have sworn Harry was snoring the tune to Oh Holy Night.

Last night was so special and writing about it so fun that I didn't move from the desk for over two hours. During that time I was interrupted twice by my mother and father who came in to tease me because they thought it was funny that I was sitting there in my pj's writing away like a little Charles Dickens which is what my father called me. Harry was real nice about keeping quiet once he woke up and started getting ready for nine o'clock mass. He even came over to pat me on the head once and say Merry Christmas, little brother. When he left for mass with his face shiny from Old Spice (which was a Christmas present), and his hair slicked back in a big wave, I was just about finished with my story.

It only takes me twenty minutes to wash up and brush my teeth and get dressed, and I couldn't eat anything because I wanted to Receive, so by twenty after nine I was sitting out in the living room with nothing to do. I could feel Little Limbo creeping up on me. It was a sunny and warm day and the living room was very bright. It was more like an Easter morning than it was like the cold and snowy way you'd hope for Christmas to be. We had opened our presents last night after everyone left and now they were laying there in their boxes. All of mine were real nice (Clue, the red sweater, the belt, the Converse, the basketball, and especially the green and gold football helmet) but I couldn't bring myself to do anything more than sit and stare at them.

I walked over to the window and pulled the curtain back. South Street was jammed with families. I looked down towards Hancock, and I thought of Wake and the weird afternoon I saw him following Corcoran, and him being followed by Cotton. I thought of him killing Jeannie. He could have done it in a lot of ways though I couldn't think of what most of them would have been. I guess since I knew what had happened I assumed he had poisoned her. That she was sleeping and he walked quietly into her room. That he dropped the poison pill into a glass of water. I imagined that then he stopped and looked at her for a second. I didn't know if he cried but I hoped he did. Then he walked out and shut the door.

I started saying a little prayer—not to God really, more to myself. But when I thought I heard something moving behind me I got real scared as though I had been doing something really bad and I almost knocked over the tree. It was time to leave.

I was still there before mass started and had to wait for Father Hennessy who is our pastor which means that he is our shepherd. Actually, it seems like every time the pastor opens his mouth, he asks for money. He starts every sermon the same way, saying Hummm, the Good People. Then he goes on to tell everybody how evil the world is and how good they are and how much money the church collected last Sunday. And this being Christmas he had added it up for the whole year, smiling with certainty that we'd give even more this upcoming year and Hummm-ing the Good People whenever he got the chance.

I sat off to the side of the main altar in a little sort of alcove chapel. There was something about sitting where I was, tucked away from the main crowd, that made it more like I was watching people at mass than like I was at mass myself. I sat or stood or knelt with all the other people but I was always a second behind and the stupidest thing of all was that when it was time for Communion I was so busy watching the whole thing that I forgot to get up and Receive myself.

I stuck around awhile after Mass ended and the place cleared out. It was better then—quieter and dimmer and gentler and better for the real churchy kind of thinking. Before I left, I went up and lit a candle but couldn't really pray good there at the center of the church, jumping with nerves every time I heard somebody behind me.

Leaving the Loews

It was three days after Christmas and I got feeling very grey at around three o'clock. The day had just been dragging along, and what had started out all nice and blue in the morning had turned as grey as I was by the middle of the afternoon.

My father was at work as usual and my mother was up the avenue. Harry was out I didn't know where, not in the Courts which were empty no matter how many times I looked over there.

I said The hell with it and decided to go to the movies. It was the first time I'd be going by myself, but the idea of seeing Hercules Unchained instead of sitting around this empty house all day was too tempting not to do it. I went into my bank and took out two dollars. I took the Central Avenue bus to the Square and got there fifteen minutes before the movie started. The Loews is some theater. It's in the center of the whole Square and it's the biggest and oldest theater in all of Hudson County, maybe in the whole state. Just walking in is spooky. The lobby's ceiling is about a hundred feet high with yellow columns going all the way to the top. There are big twinkling chandeliers hanging from the ceiling that reflect in all the mirrors on the walls that make it look like there are dozens of them. The whole floor's covered in a thick maroon and swirling gold carpet. If you're standing at the front of the lobby with the doors and glass behind you, there's a big curving wide staircase of five steps in front of you. Off from the landing of those steps go two sets of twelve narrower stairs, one to the right, one to the left, both to the balcony.

I don't get lost because I know the Loews and I know where I'm going, but if something happened to throw me off it would take forever to figure out how to get back where I was. Not only is there upstairs and downstairs and a lobby and a theater part, but there's two balconies, an upper and lower, and a mezzanine, and side boxes like what Lincoln got shot in, and the stairways have little nooks and alcoves with fancy chairs or statues, and there's so much rich and glittery stuff everywhere you turn that it's more like you're in a haunted Vincent Price mansion than a place you'd go to watch a movie.

The theater part itself is also very, very big. Harry says that counting all the balconies they can fit four-thousand people in there. This afternoon there must have been thirty-five or forty people as best I could tell. Around the sides, they've made it look like the walls of a Roman fort. They have fake cut-stones going up about three-quarters of the way and fake centurions standing guard on top. The ceiling looks like the night sky. It's a real dark blue and they've made it look like there are a hundred stars up there including some comets. If you lean your head back and gaze up, you'd swear it was real.

Today was my third time to see Hercules Unchained. It's an Italian movie with the words dubbed in. It's neat to look at because it's in Technicolor and Panavision—in other words the colors are super bold and the screen is extra big—and because of where and when it takes place which is the ancient Mediterranean Sea as they explain at the beginning of the movie. There are a lot of good, exciting scenes in it, too. There's one where the Slave

Queen softens Hercules' brain then tries to rip out his heart, and there's another one where this tribe of men as hairy as apes chain his arms to two white stallions that try to pull him apart.

My all-time favorite scene is at the end. After beating all these enemies, Hercules is unchained again. He walks to the edge of a rocky cliff and overlooks the sea. The yellow sunshine is drenching everything—the white rocks, the wooden ships, the blue sky, and the blue-green waters. Hercules puts one foot up on a rock and puts his hands on his waist. The breeze blows back his hair and he just stands there breathing—Hrrrr—hufrrrrr, which is also dubbed in. Big music starts up and you get further and further away from Hercules who gets smaller and smaller and smaller, and you know exactly how Hercules feels there right smack in the middle of his own great place.

When the movie was over, I walked through the lobby and I looked out the front door and I was amazed! Not only was it dark out, which I should have expected but didn't, but it was snowing and everything was covered. I walked out the glass doors of the Loews and heard the noise of all the people and of the traffic and I smelled the snow and the car fumes and tasted the cold, cold air. For a second I couldn't move. Everything in Journal Square, the stores, the buses, the sky, the people and the buildings were so different from this afternoon.   I thought of the blue light and I noticed it right at the same time. I was only four or five years old the first time I ever noticed it. It was one of those things that you remembered and forgot. Even though the Square at night in the snow and blue light was beautiful, I was getting spooked by it because I knew that I knew where the blue light was coming from but I couldn't remember or find it. I looked to the top of the billboards which I figured was a reasonable place it might be, but, no, it wasn't on any of them. Then I'd think that I'd remembered. I looked on top of the Jersey Journal Building, it wasn't there. I looked on top of the Stanley and on top of the Port Authority Building and on top of the Trust Company, but there was no blue light shining from any of them. I was really confused. I looked up at the clock, half frosted in snow. No blue light.

I scratched my head and laughed at myself for not knowing what I always knew, but laughing didn't ease me and I could feel some kind of worries coming on.

I looked to the bus-transit island in the middle of the Square and there was the Central Avenue bus loading up. I jumped out into the slush in the middle of traffic and ran for it. I caught up just as it was pulling out and banged on its side—like a real frantic nut. The driver stopped and let me on. What are you doing running after a bus like that, son. It's an excellent way to get yourself killed.

I took a seat in the back corner and I hate to say it but I was shaking. I couldn't wait to be home and all cuddled in the comfort of my own damn living room.

Monk

Beginning with the time I left the movies and for the past two days things have been really, really bad and I almost believe that something weird was going on when I left the Loews, a feeling telling me that something very horrible was happening at that very moment when I was all a mess about the blue light, etc. There was another killing and it's made such a mess of me that I haven't been able to get back to being my old self. My mother and father can tell and have been very nice—my father poking me in the ribs every time I pass him, and, when we watch TV, my mother spending more time looking at me than she does looking at the program.

Wake killed Corcoran early Thursday night. Wake shot him, shot him twice. I feel sad about it because now I know that Wake will never be better, and who knows what it'll do to Cotton.

On Friday, Harry bought as many different newspapers as he could get his hands on, even going up to the Transfer Station to get some out of town ones, and made a scrapbook from the articles. The Jersey Journal and the Hudson Dispatch being the two most local papers are the two with the biggest headline stories. But it was really all over, in the New York papers and even on the TV news.

He shot him twice. Somehow, he got Corcoran down in his apartment and killed him. He shot him once in the heart and once in the head. The shot to the heart was probably the first and killing one.

The Hudson Dispatch had a picture of Wake's cellar apartment with nobody in it, not Wake and not Corcoran's body, just arrows pointing to the blood splattered on the chair and on the wall. Next to it was an article called Portrait of a Killer. In the Jersey Journal there was a picture that had been taken last summer after their outing to Lincoln Park. It was a picture of the whole gang of them all together, arms around one another's shoulders. My father was in the picture, pointing at me standing behind the photographer, and Joe McGill and Mr. Caruso and Cotton were in the picture along with Wake. They had drawn a circle around Wake's head to identify him. He was resting his chin on Cotton's shoulder, smiling and waving and as happy as I've ever seen him.

And there wasn't just one article. There was one about Mrs. Parish and about how she screamed and battled and collapsed. There was one about Cotton where he was trying to describe what Wake was like. All over the place there were articles. In all the papers, articles with the names of people I knew and pictures of places I've spent every day of my life. Harry cut them out and scotch-taped them next to one another in his scrapbook where they'd stay for ever and ever until one day they'll be as faded yellow as Pearl Harbor Day and little bits of them will fall off every time you open the book.

After I read all the stories, I went down to B&J's and sat by myself at the end of the bar. There was a pinch-hitter tending bar, someone I didn't know, and some of the other guys told him it was okay to serve me a coke. Joe McGill had come in to set up the free beans and franks like he does every Friday afternoon. Things didn't seem different enough to me. All the guys looked the same in their caps and shirts and coats in a row down the bar. The place smelled the same, of whiskey and beer and cigarettes and wet cardboard and hot radiators and the franks and beans. The sounds, too, were exactly the same.

The pinch-hitter gave me the soda and pushed my quarter back at me. Sitting there, all I was trying to do was be myself, just my old self, but I could tell by the way guys were winking and smiling at me that I was wearing my trouble on my puss. So I sat there pretending everything was normal not even knowing if everybody else was pretending or not. It was very hard to figure out what had changed and what hadn't because the answer to both was everything. My head still ached and I felt warm and a little green around the gills. From the end of the bar, I had the same weird feeling as I had on Christmas morning at mass, that as much as being in the bar I was watching people being in the bar, as though living was starting to feel like writing.

It was three o'clock when I left B&J's and headed for Ogden Avenue. Ogden is the last block in our neighborhood before the hill down to Hoboken. The Hill is another place I know real well and know all the safe paths from the ones you don't want to go near, and I know all its landmarks like Cobble Road and the White Wall and Piss Creek and I'm SURE that I'll still know them even when I'm sixty.

I went to my favorite spot, a wide, flat rock straight down from North Street where you could walk around without being afraid you were going to fall off. It was a real icy and breezy day, so clear that I could make out the individual windows in the Empire State Building. All New York City was out there, from the George Washington Bridge to my left to the Statue of Liberty to my right. Straight down below me, at the bottom of the Hill, were the railroad tracks, then Hoboken, then the river.

It's usually not the winter but the summer that we all come over the Hill. The easiest way down is the Hundred Steps which is probably missing a dozen of its hundred but the most missing is two in a row and it's not that hard to jump. One time because of that instead of calling it the Hundred Steps, Harry called it the Missing Steps and then Boo called it the Missing Links and that's what we called it last summer until I guess September when we started calling it Vincent because everybody says that Vincent Scolero resembles the missing link. It's not that funny, I guess.

I like it down there, over the Hill, I always have, since I was little. Like two and a half summers ago Harry and Boo brought me down for the first time and taught me how to smoke Winston's which Boo called their cigarette of choice. For the whole month of June him and Harry held like classes for me and Franny and Mo. They taught us how to inhale and talk without losing smoke and how to exhale through the nose without gagging and how to blow smoke rings. Then there was another time, two days after Fourth of July, when we were getting chased by a whole gang of kids from Hoboken until we ran into another group of our friends and then wound up chasing them. In the mess of running up and down the cliffs, one of Franny's jumps was short and he landed in a ditch and busted his leg and an ambulance had to come to take him away. Another time, I hitched a train with Harry that we took all the way to West New York.

Friday, yesterday, was the first time I'd been back down here since September. There used to be a Spiffy Whiffle Ball factory right below where I was standing, but they knocked it down since the summer. All that's left is pigeons and rubble and hundreds of red and white whiffle ball boxes blowing around in circles.

I climbed back up into the neighborhood. The wind was icy sharp as I climbed South Street towards my house. I hated the wind and I liked hating it. I cursed it and I thought of nothing but that, nothing but how I hated how hard it was coming at me. I cursed the wind, I fought it, I hated it. When I finally made it back to B&J's, I was frozen stiff. I sat in the hall on the bottom step with the bar off to my left and the doorway to the outside in front of me. I could hear all the chatter from the bar and, coming from past that, the far-away yells from the Courts. I chewed on a fingernail as I looked out the doorway. From between my teeth, I spit the nail into a 7up carton. I walked over to the entrance and I braced my hands against the sides and poked out my head. I just looked up and down the block. Everything seemed pretty okay.

I went back to the steps and let out a little sigh, maybe more a phew than a sigh. I don't ever want my head to get any tighter. I don't even want it to stay as tight as it's been. It's been sick, mostly. Sick and run down like I've got the brain flu. I know I've got to be easy on myself and all but I really hope it hurries and gets back to usual because I do not want to walk around with this headache for the rest of my life however long that may be.

On the Writing of *As Told by Monk*

I began writing *As Told By Monk* when I was 27 and completed it when I was 29, or something like that. (From here on, I'll pretend to remember specific dates, but really I don't.) When I wrote *Monk,* I was living in Somerville, Massachusetts—had already been there a few years. I was using that chunk of my life to see if I could make a writer of myself, so one of my goals was to avoid a real or full-time job but still make enough money to live on.

I spent the winter of '80-'81 working temp jobs in the Boston area (these were secretarial temp placements, since the only job skill of any sort I had was that I could type 50 words per minute). Consequently, I've ever since been able to include on my resume that I worked at Harvard, MIT, Tufts, Boston University, and the Boston Museum of Modern Art. So, I spent that winter working those jobs and writing *Monk.* The good thing about those temp jobs was that you could pretty much dictate your own schedule, and the worst thing that could happen would be that you wound up with an extra day off here or there.

Most of the actual writing of *As Told by Monk* took place at Harvard—in Loker Reading Room at Widener Library. I would hand write there for a few hours in the morning, then return to Somerville (either walk or take the 77) and type/edit what I'd written. Later, I'd head back to Widener and line-edit my newly typed version and begin working on the next chapter. At night, there was a good chance I'd hand over the day's product to my girlfriend in the hope of some praise, following the same or similar routine day after day.

By the time the summer of 1980 came around, I had submitted a number of Monk's short chapters to a bunch of literary magazines, and although I was new to publishing I already had enough experience to know that I was getting far more acceptances than was typical. One of the magazines nominated "Blessed in Latin," I think, for a Pushcart. My friends' enthusiasm was great and genuine. But, of course, as for getting it published as a book, no luck. I had the belief that my writing was outside the mainstream. I don't really know whether or not this is true, but if it was, I believed it had nothing to do with being experimental and a lot to do with the fact that I saw myself as more of a folk or naïve artist than a trained one. Even though I had a Masters Degree in Creative Writing from Goddard College, I saw myself as an unsophisticated and under-educated kid from Jersey City relative to the worlds of literature and Cambridge. Which is not to say I thought I was inferior. Not at all, just that I wasn't one of them.

In the spring I was assigned a temp job at the Harvard Graduate School of Design—it was the week the pope got shot. I did well enough there—I showed up on time and did what I was told—that they hired me for the summer. I think I was the assistant to the assistant to the Director of the GSD's Continuing Education Program. I got to know the people I worked with and I told them about my writing. My boss gave me the key to the office so I could come back at night and type in book form and clean type a copy of *Monk* I'd self-publish. With great nostalgia and pride, I remember walking back to Harvard Square those May and June and July evenings. Having previously worked at Gnomon Copy, I had connections in a place that mattered. So, after typing, then cutting, then pasting the 159 pages of *Monk*, I devised a cover and found a book bindery. By the end of September I had two boxes full of books—200 with yellow covers, 100 with grey.

I used my prestige with Gnomon Copy to have a bunch of flyers made up. I was pretty clever about it, or thought I was. The first time I put up the flyers—all of them in the Harvard Square area—all that was written on them were the words "As Told By Monk." (Ah, the mystery. Must have had everyone in Cambridge wondering!) A week later, I went back with a second barrage—these making clear that *Monk* was a book and including some compliments I'd gotten from a couple of literary magazines. (I still cannot accept that a cop had the nerve to give me a ticket for taping them up—I forget what the ordinance was. In 1980, as you walked through Harvard Square it would have been impossible to directly touch a wall; all were covered with announcements, broadsides, or ads for apartments "sought" or "available.")

Anyway, there it was: *As Told By Monk*, my book. I stopped in all the Cambridge bookstores, and maybe one or two in Boston, where the folks in charge were willing to sell the book on consignment. In most cases, the stores put them on display. One store, WordsWorth, had my book right up by the counter. Reading International, on the other hand, just put the books on the fiction shelves, and there I was between Colette and Conrad. I think I sold the book for $4.00 and got back $2.40 on each sale.

And my goodness, here I am 33-years later.

When I decided to re-release *Monk*, the first decision I made was not to mess around with it very much. There are a few minor changes here and there, but I wanted to make sure I didn't impose my 60-year-old wisdom on my 28-year-old inventiveness. It had to remain a book written by a guy in his twenties. So, the book is today what it was in 1980. It's remarkable to me how close I still feel to the text. Time after time after time, after reading the first few words of a sentence I could complete it without looking back at the original. I laughed in the same places and was still dissatisfied at the same spots. I'm also glad I stuck with my original decision to include no question marks or quotation marks. The lack of quotation marks makes sense: I didn't want any points of separation between the reader and Monk's voice. The refusal to use question marks is at least 50% due to stubbornness.

I'm happy that I have been able to give my dear friend and long-time partner Monk a second life.

ABOUT THE AUTHOR

Joe Colicchio has two other previously published novels: *High Gate Health and Beauty* (Creative Arts Publishing, 2000) which was named a top-ten novel of the year by the web-reviewer MostlyFiction.com; and *The Trouble with Mental Wellness* (Bridge Works Publishing, 2004), selected as a recommended book by *Library Journal*. Joe has completed two residencies at Virginia Center for the Creative Arts, received two Geraldine R. Dodge Grants, and two New Jersey State Council on the Arts Grants, including the Distinguished Artist Award, the highest the state bestows. Joe is an Associate Professor of English at Hudson County Community College in Jersey City, NJ.

ACKNOWLEDGEMENTS

Front cover design – Jack Colicchio
Cover formatting and back cover design -
Jeffrey Nixon, www.jeffinteractive.com
Back cover photography – Patricia Vogler

Made in the USA
Middletown, DE
25 February 2016